They shone blue-white in the darkness (page 125)

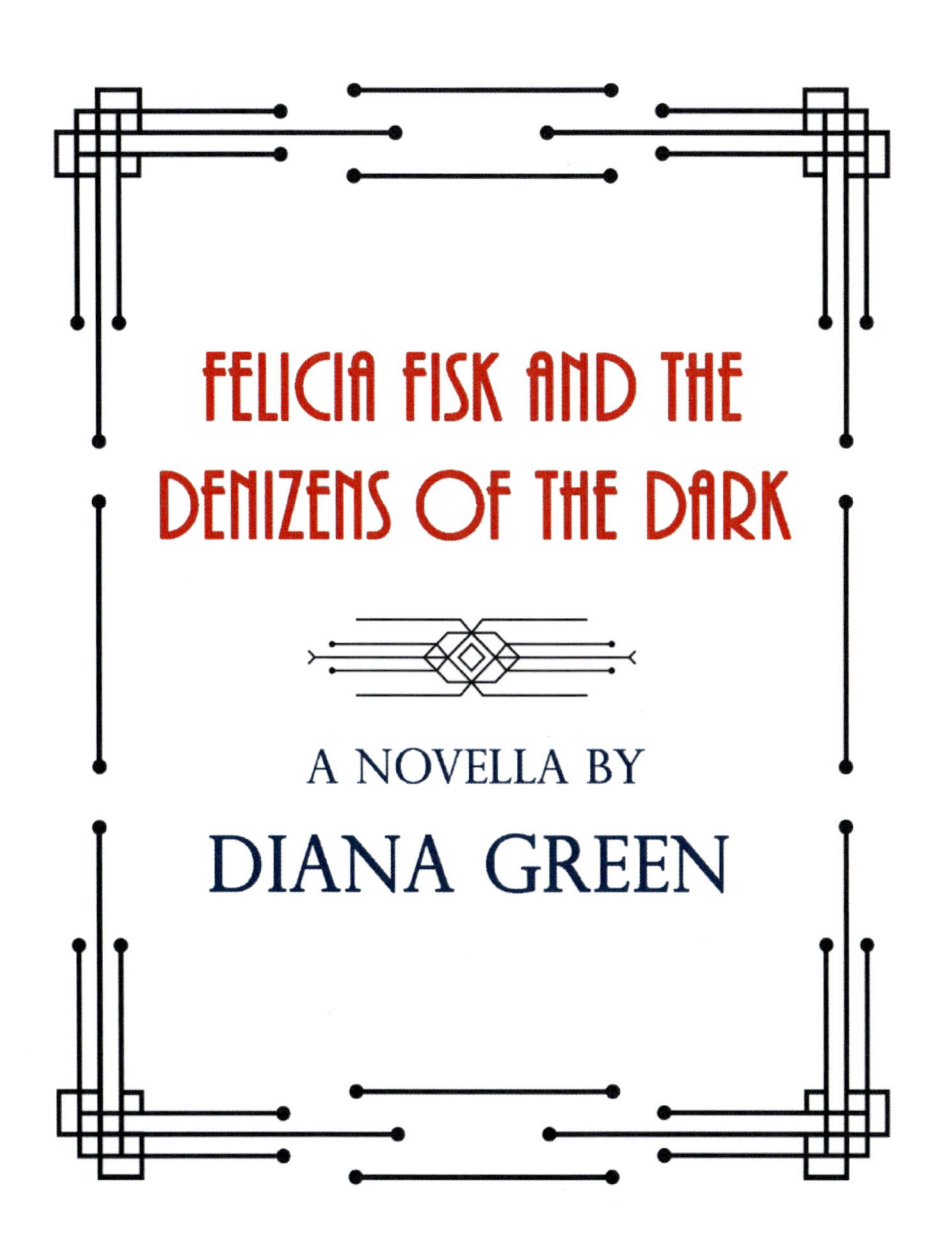

FELICIA FISK AND THE DENIZENS OF THE DARK

A NOVELLA BY
DIANA GREEN

This is a work of fiction. Names, characters, places, and incidents are either the product of the author's imagination or are used fictitiously, and any resemblance to actual persons living or dead, business establishments, events, or locales, is coincidental.

Felicia Fisk and the Denizens of the Dark

Copyright © 2023 Diana Green

All rights reserved. No part of this book may be used or reproduced in any manner whatsoever without written permission of the author.

Interior and cover design by Diana Green
cover art and illustrations purchased from
iStock.com
artist Tithi Luadthong

http://www.istockphoto.com/portfolio/Grandfailure?mediatype=illustration

https://tithi-luadthong.pixels.com

TABLE OF CONTENTS

CHAPTER ONE	11
CHAPTER TWO	22
CHAPTER THREE	38
CHAPTER FOUR	50
CHAPTER FIVE	64
CHAPTER SIX	79
CHAPTER SEVEN	94
CHAPTER EIGHT	106
CHAPTER NINE	119
CHAPTER TEN	129

LIST OF ILLUSTRATIONS

They shone blue-white in the darkness	*Frontispiece*
A humble cottage along the tidewater	16
He searched everywhere in our world	20
Fisk Hall—a grand old brick mansion	23
They dove deep to the river bottom	29
Running along the smooth golden beach	33
Dark tentacles writhed on its skull-like head	36
There was something uncanny about the man	44
Fine mist wrapped the falls like a white veil	48
The whole warding began to break down	53
Memories of lazy afternoons spent reading	58
The Tree offered up a piece of its heart	62
Monstrous pincers burst from his right arm	67
It towered above any neighbors	76
Their eyes glowed bright as embers	81
Perched precariously over rushing falls	86

They must have numbered in the hundreds	*90*
Red and black speckled its armored hide	*95*
The rider appeared to be a young Human woman	*99*
A glory of tall towers and delicate spires	*102*
The image was arresting, at least fifty feet high	*112*
Symbols lit with white fire, as the center opened	*117*
The wooden tenements looked slapped together	*121*
She needed one hand free to hold a glow globe	*128*
Cedric laughed gleefully, unafraid for his safety	*137*
She saw everything in dagger-sharp clarity	*134*
Her aunt stood regal as a queen	*139*
And so they lived wholeheartedly ever after	*143*

FELICIA FISK AND THE DENIZENS OF THE DARK

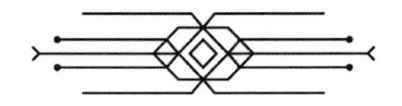

CHAPTER ONE

Felicia Fisk was not well pleased, upon waking at 3:40 am, to find a diminutive individual poking her with a spear the size of a shrimp fork. He stood glowering by her pillow, shining with orange luminescence. A coil of vapor wafted from his nostrils, smelling faintly of vinegar and burned garlic.

Blinking, Felicia pushed the little spear away and sat up, taking a closer look at her assailant. The creature resembled a furry tangerine, with stocky limbs, curved horns, and glowing yellow eyes. His wide mouth revealed serrated fangs and a crimson forked tongue, which flicked like a snake's.

"Now, what is this all about?" Felicia asked, failing to disguise the irritation in her voice.

You might expect someone in her situation to show greater surprise. But Felicia was not an ordinary woman. She had been raised in a family of sorcerers, with knowledge of the secret realms.

Despite living in the modern era, with motorcars, radios, air conditioners, and other conveniences becoming widely available—not to mention women finally able to wear trousers in public—Felicia knew of older stranger realities that existed alongside the mundane world. The fact that she had turned her back, most forcefully, on all such matters did not mean those matters kept their backs turned on her. Sometimes, unfortunately, they popped up and required attention.

"I demand satisfaction for the wrongs perpetrated by your uncle, Horace Randolph Martin Fisk, against my family." The tiny monster ended his pronouncement with a dramatic growl, waving the spear in Felicia's direction.

She sighed and rubbed the bridge of her nose, aware of a burgeoning headache. Of course this involved her uncle. The man cast a long shadow, even after his death.

"I will hear your claims, but I'm not sure how much satisfaction is possible." She made an effort at courtesy, despite growing misgivings. This nocturnal visitor probably had good cause for outrage. Uncle Horace had been an unrepentant swindler, known for his dirty dealings throughout the realms.

"Before we proceed, though, may I ask how you passed through my wardings? I assumed my home was safe from unexpected visitors."

"Your talismans are out of date and need replacing," the creature explained. "I simply found a crack and slipped through."

"Oh. Indeed?" Felicia felt a glimmer of embarrassment. She needed to pay better attention to these things.

It was just so easy to forget—caught up as she was in a common life—spending her days among those who knew nothing of magic and hidden worlds.

"I demand satisfaction," the intruder repeated. "Justice must be served!"

"Yes. So you said. Shall we be civilized and discuss things over biscuits and tea?"

"Only a fool takes food and drink from a sorcerer. I have been warned."

"Sage advice, but I am not a sorcerer. I'm a librarian. My hospitality is quite harmless, and I shall need fortification if we're to discuss blood debts at this hour of the morning. You're welcome to join me or not, as you see fit."

"What is a librarian?"

"I take care of books and make them available for people to borrow. There is nothing nefarious about it. You're perfectly safe drinking my tea."

He shook his head. "My task is too important. I can't risk falling for any Human tricks."

"Suit yourself."

Felicia rose from bed, donned slippers and dressing gown, then went to put the kettle on. She glanced back to see the creature clamber down her bedpost and trot along the hall behind her. He moved surprisingly fast for someone only three inches tall.

Once the kettle was heating, she reached a special tin of chocolate biscuits down from the high shelf. Facing the prospect of hashing out her uncle's crimes, she felt a little indulgence was warranted. Perhaps chocolate would help sweeten the unpleasant task.

A loud splash outside startled her, and she hurried through the kitchen door onto the narrow deck that overhung the river. Less than a year ago, a man had fallen into the water, just three cottages down the row from hers. He'd been drinking heavily and drowned before anyone knew what happened.

The pointless tragedy of it disturbed Felicia, who sometimes took care of the man's young son—when the widowed mother worked evenings. If only someone had realized a person was dying just a few yards from their back door, he might have been saved. Ever since, Felicia had been vigilant. She investigated any unusual sounds or possible signs of trouble.

On this occasion, nothing appeared to be wrong. The only evidence of disturbance was an expanding circle of ripples, moving over the glassy surface of the river. Likely some neighbor had thrown an unwanted household item into the water, rather than disposing of it properly. Such things weren't uncommon in the area where Felicia lived.

Despite being the sole remaining member of the once wealthy Fisk family, she'd barely inherited enough to pay for an education. With only a librarian's salary, she required modest accommodations—not easy to find in a popular seaside town like Port Lorence. Renting a humble cottage along the tidewater had proven to be the answer.

Here, so close to the estuary, the river moved at a leisurely pace, spreading out wide and smooth. At low tide, the heavy smell of mudflats hung over the neighborhood, but tonight a fresh salt breeze brushed Felicia's face, whispering through her hair. She took a moment to drink it in, calmed by the smell of the sea, the distant cry of gulls, and the gentle lap of water under the wooden planks she stood on.

For the briefest instant she glimpsed something slipping silently by in the river. It looked too large for a fish and too narrow for a porpoise or freshwater shark. But it moved with the sinuous grace of an aquatic predator.

Her skin prickled cold. Were other supernatural creatures abroad tonight, in addition to her uninvited guest? Surely not. A bustling Human town was no place for visitors from the secret realms. This must simply be her overtired brain inventing shadows.

The screeching kettle called her back inside, to prepare a cup of tea, just the way she liked it, with exactly an ounce of milk and a half teaspoon of sugar.

"Are you sure you won't take refreshment?" she asked her visitor, who stood near the salt and pepper shakers at the center of her kitchen table.

He frowned. "I'm sure. This is no frivolous matter, and I won't be put off any longer."

A humble cottage along the tidewater

"Of course." She sat and sipped her tea.

"Felicia Renata Annabelle Fisk, as the only surviving close relative of Horace Randolph Martin Fisk, I hold you responsible in making amends for your uncle's crimes, which include both vile thievery and foulest murder."

"Murder? That's considerably worse than expected." Felicia closed her eyes a moment, attempting to tamp down the anxiety pressing on her chest. This was precisely the sort of thing she'd tried to avoid for so long—reminders of her past and the shadows lurking there.

She'd done her best to put it all behind her, choosing not to think about magic, other worlds, or her family's legacy. That, no doubt, explained her negligence in maintaining the wardings around her home, when everything else in the cottage was neat as a pin.

"Felicia Renata Annabelle Fisk, do you acknowledge that Horace Randolph Martin—"

"Wait. Before we go any further, can you please just call me Felicia? And refer to my uncle simply as Horace? Otherwise this could take all night." Her family had been fond of piling the names of dead relatives onto every new arrival. It was an added bother she did not need right now.

"Very well," the creature conceded. "In that case you may call me by a shortened version of my name."

"Which is?"

"In full, I am The Great and Terrible Xtholubahn Nemurithain Brathoss. But you may call me The Great and Terrible."

"Isn't that more of an epithet?"

"No!" He huffed in offense. "The Great and Terrible is my personal name, earned with a coming of age quest. Before that time I was merely Number Eight Xtholubahn Nemurithain Brathoss."

"You were eighth born of your siblings?"

"Yes. We have large families, but many of our young die before coming of age. So we wait for personal names to be earned, once survival seems likely."

"May I ask what the other names mean?"

"Xtholubahn is the name of my particular family, and Nemurithain is my clan. The Brathoss are all of my kind, who live in various clanholds around the Dark Realm."

"Ah, the Dark Realm. I remember reading about it as a girl. But I don't recall any mention of the Brathoss."

"We keep to ourselves and carefully hide our clanholds...for self-defense." He cleared his throat uncomfortably. "Despite being among the fiercest and most ancient inhabitants of the Dark Realm, we are also among the smallest. Some would take advantage of our modest stature. Therefore, we exercise caution."

"That sounds wise." Felicia sensed his embarrassment and sought to ease it. "You must have completed a very dangerous coming of age quest, to earn *The Great and Terrible* as a name."

"It was perilous, yes." He puffed up a little, his eyes brightening. "I slew a pernicious ukluff and took its venom sack. We use the poison on the tips of our spears."

"I hope *that* spear wasn't dipped in venom." Felicia pointed at the weapon resting in his furry orange hands. "You poked me with it earlier."

He shook his head. "I didn't come here to kill you, only to demand restitution. You wouldn't be much use dead."

"That is reassuring, I suppose." She sighed and rubbed her aching temples. "Well, we'd best get on with it. Please explain your grievances, and I'll see what can be done."

"Seven years ago, your uncle came hunting for the Crown of Visions, my clan's greatest treasure. He searched everywhere in our world, through the Chrysolite Forest, the Dagger Glades, the Graytooth Mountains, and even the Caverns of Floating Death, until he found our clanhold. Somehow, he managed to subdue our gatekeeper with sorcery and then stole the Crown of Visions. In the process, he brutally murdered our chief and her consort, who were also my parents."

The Great and Terrible's voice wobbled. "I was not yet full grown, but my older siblings died trying to defend our family. Only myself and two younger sisters survived."

Felicia found herself momentarily speechless. She had known her uncle was selfish, dishonest, and prone to larceny. He'd even killed a rival sorcerer once, in a duel. But this! To slaughter an innocent family! How could he do such a thing?

He searched everywhere in our world

"I see my story comes as a shock," The Great and Terrible observed. "You were not aware of your uncle's true nature?"

She took a deep breath and then another, trying to remain calm. What The Great and Terrible asked was far from simple to answer. On the surface—in her conscious mind—she believed Horace was nothing but a petty villain, a greedy conniving charlatan who put his own ambitions above the welfare of others.

Yet buried deep inside her, locked away with all the unresolved grief, rage, and fear, lay darker suspicions. Had he been involved in her parents' deaths? Was the reckless 'accident' that killed her aunt actually premeditated?

These thoughts had tormented Felicia in the past, but she'd turned away from them, unable to confront the overwhelming emotions they raised. Now, hearing The Great and Terrible's story, those depths within her churned. The carefully maintained barriers shuddered and memories came seeping up, refusing to be denied.

CHAPTER TWO

Felicia remembered the day, during her seventh summer, when Uncle Horace first truly frightened her. Until then he'd been merely an enigma, funny and attentive, when the mood struck him, but without warning turning harsh and dismissive. As the youngest of three siblings—and uncommonly magically gifted—he'd been doted on as a child, leading to a strong sense of entitlement. Adding this to his callous ambitious nature, the result was a decidedly difficult man.

Horace lived with Felicia and her parents, Ambrose and Renata, at the ancestral estate, Fisk Hall—a grand old brick mansion, surrounded by three hundred acres of meadow and forest. The place had fallen into decline as the family fortunes dwindled, but it proved a veritable paradise for a child like Felicia. She loved the overgrown gardens and woods, the fish pond, and nearby river. They offered a never ending feast for her imagination.

Fisk Hall—a grand old brick mansion

No one bothered about how she spent her days. Mable, the one remaining servant, barely kept up with the mountain of housework, and Felicia's parents had more important matters to attend to. The truth was, they seemed disappointed in their plain quiet daughter.

Although Felicia received her mother's coloring—dark hair and hazel eyes—she lacked Renata's beauty. From the tall, fair Fisks she inherited nothing but height, which merely served to make her a lanky awkward child.

Worse still was Felicia's meager magical talent. The only skill she demonstrated was sensing the presence of sorcery. On a good day she could catch glimmers of a particular enchantment's purpose and once or twice managed to dismantle a spell. But she couldn't cast even the simplest charms herself.

In truth, undoing or "breaking" sorcery was a rare gift, by no means easy to manifest. But Felicia's parents saw little merit in it. As the offspring of two venerable sorcerous lineages, they had hoped for better—something more in line with Horace's astonishing mastery of illusions and telekinesis. Now those were talents to impress!

Over the years, Felicia witnessed her uncle's acts of cruelty and deceit with growing uneasiness, but her parents never seemed to notice his transgressions. Her father—Horace's older brother—was especially fond of him. The one time Felicia expressed concerns, Ambrose grew angry and scolded her for being a silly tattletale, who had no business finding fault with her elders. He praised Horace's genius, which apparently excused all of sorts of erratic behavior.

Aunt Althea, the middle Fisk sibling, proved the only one bothered by Horace's antics. They butted heads on multiple occasions, but Ambrose invariably took his brother's side. This created an uncomfortable rift, driving the family apart.

Althea's kind, down-to-earth nature stood in stark contrast to the rest of the family, which may have explained why she chose not to live with them. Felicia liked her aunt and might have confided in her. But Althea visited less and less often, busy with her position as an archeology professor at Wexhill University. She sometimes left the country for months at a time—working on excavations—as was the case that fateful summer when Felicia turned seven.

Horace's behavior had become especially volatile, his eyes seeming to burn with unnatural intensity. Felicia observed him sneaking out of the house at odd hours, often with mysterious bundles in hand. She also caught him studying her parents, an unpleasant appraising look on his face, as if his family were nothing but curious lab specimens.

On the day in question, she'd been reading—tucked away in the woods near the river—when Horace came slinking by, seeming oblivious to her. She watched him pass, then impulsively rose and followed.

They walked for nearly an hour, beyond the part of the estate Felicia was familiar with.

She crept along behind, careful not to make a sound, wondering where he could possibly be going. Her uncle wasn't known for enjoying long nature hikes.

The gentle sounds of the river became more forceful—a rushing that was almost a roar—indicating sizable rapids or falls lay ahead. Felicia leaned over the bank, peering ahead through the trees, trying to see where Horace led her.

As if responding to some silent cue he stopped, and she ducked behind a bush for cover. Her uncle flicked a hand past his cheek and ear, as one might wave away a pesky bug. Felicia flew backwards, struck with an invisible force so powerful it flung her into the middle of the river.

Here the water ran deep and cold, stealing her breath away. She flailed, trying to slow her descent toward the river bottom, but the strength with which she'd been hurled was too great. Down she plummeted, terror taking hold, as her empty lungs screamed for air.

Thankfully, in that moment, strong arms gripped her around the waist, hauling her up to the surface and out on the river bank. She coughed up water, crying and shivering with shock. Her mysterious rescuer withdrew to a safe distance, watching warily. Uncle Horace, meanwhile, was nowhere to be seen.

Although of similar size and shape to Felicia, the person who saved her certainly wasn't Human. Scales in varying hues of blue, green, and bronze covered much of her body, with the skin between a dark iridescent copper. Her eyes resembled a cat's, her hair like slick waterweed. Webbing stretched between her elongated fingers and toes.

Once Felicia calmed down enough to speak, she introduced herself and thanked the strange river girl, whose name was Islen. She was one of the Nyarra, a water-loving people who dwelt near lakes and rivers in the subterranean Dark Realm.

Nyarra rarely visited the surface world anymore, but Islen was uncommonly adventurous. Since she was little, she'd listened with fascination to tales of vast oceans, blue sunlit skies, and the mysterious ways of Humans. Her heart was set on exploration.

Although she was only two years older than Felicia, her parents considered her capable of caring for herself and making her own decisions. This astonishing freedom was typical for Nyarran children—after they'd reached nine or ten years of age, and all their scales had grown in. They were considered independent at that stage, even to the point of building their own separate dwellings, if they wished.

This in no way diminished the strong familial bonds that held Nyarran communities together. Parents, Grandparents, Aunts, and Uncles all still showered the young with love and advice. They simply gave them the right to make their own choices. And Islen chose to explore.

Over that summer the two girls became close—Islen being Felicia's only friend, since she'd never been allowed to attend school or join activities at the local village. How wonderful to find a kindred spirit with whom to share her days. She loved reading to Islen, who had an insatiable appetite for stories. In turn, the Nyarran girl took Felicia on marvelous aquatic adventures.

By kissing both Felicia's eyelids and her mouth, Islen could impart a temporary ability to see clearly underwater and hold her breath for many minutes at a time. Hands clasped together, they dove deep to the river bottom, chasing fish, searching for treasures, and watching as boats passed by overhead.

One day Islen showed her where Uncle Horace went on his mysterious excursions. Upstream from the spot Felicia had been thrown into the river was a large falls, at least twenty feet high and thirty across. Boulders formed a natural jetty out into the water, where Horace would pass under the falls to a hidden tunnel or chamber.

Islen had seen him go that way several times, but she never followed farther. She could sense something rotten about the man and cautioned Felicia to be careful of him.

It was a warning that didn't need repeating. After Horace had propelled Felicia into the river—with a mere flick of his fingers—she'd given him a wide berth. Nothing was ever said about the incident, but she understood her uncle's message loud and clear. Keep out of his business or else!

They dove deep to the river bottom

Felicia never tried to enter Horace's lair behind the falls. It was sure to be guarded with powerful wardings, and she feared arousing his anger. Despite her curiosity about the place, investigating seemed too risky.

Instead she focused on the friendship and fun Islen brought to her lonely life. The weeks seemed to fly by, as they met often at the river, picnicking, swimming, playing, and whiling away the sweet golden days.

All too soon her idyllic summer ended. In late August Felicia's parents died in a car accident. Apparently the brakes had given out, along a perilous stretch of mountain road.

Fisk Hall became an alien and foreboding place, with the clocks all stopped at the hour of the tragedy, and black cloth draped over every mirror and window. Mable quit as soon as she heard the news, unwilling to have Horace as her master. That left Felicia alone with her uncle and also alone with her grief.

Although she had never been close to her parents, their sudden deaths were deeply distressing—made all the more so by Horace's looming presence. He paid little attention to Felicia, but now he was her guardian. That fact added a shadow of threat and uncertainty to an already upsetting situation.

She spent most of her time hiding away, trying not to catch Horace's notice, till a week later her aunt arrived, having left her archeological dig the same day she received the terrible news.

Althea quickly put things in order, insisting she take over guardianship of Felicia. Horace didn't protest, as he had no desire to raise a child. But he did clash vigorously with his sister over the will. He wanted Fisk Hall for himself and was prepared to fight tooth and claw to keep it.

In the end Althea surrendered the estate. It was easier to let Horace have what he wanted—especially as she had a decent income from the University and her own little house in the town of Wexhill.

It was there she took Felicia, fixing up a pretty bedroom for her, and making every effort to be welcoming. Althea even cut back her work schedule, to ensure she had time for her niece.

And so Felicia's life changed drastically. Until now she'd been mostly solitary, her education consisting of a few primary lessons from her parents and permission to read anything in the Fisk Hall library. Now she attended public school, with children her own age. Although this sometimes felt like a mixed blessing—as she remained a shy and awkward girl—there was no doubt her situation had improved.

Althea proved to be a caring guardian, taking a keen interest in Felicia's daily life and wellbeing. She introduced her niece to the joys of bird watching, baking, knitting, and of course archeology. Althea encouraged Felicia's passion for books, and also helped hone her talent for sensing magic and 'breaking' sorceries.

They never visited Uncle Horace, a fact for which Felicia felt grateful. Instead she and her aunt traveled during school holidays, including a fortnight spent each summer at Port Lorence enjoying the seaside.

Felicia dearly loved the ocean. Running along the smooth golden beach, eating ice creams on the pier, standing in the sparkling shallows, with the sky spread above, and the endless azure waves rolling in—at such times she knew an all-encompassing joy. Her life felt bright and beautiful, full of wondrous possibilities.

Often she wished to share these experiences with Islen but never saw the Nyarran girl again. No river ran through Wexhill, and even if one did, it wouldn't be safe for Islen to visit a Human town. Beyond that, Felicia had no way of contacting her to share the news of moving to a new home. In truth, The Dark Realm might as well have been the other side of the moon.

And so their time together began to seem like an improbable dream, lovely but increasingly distant. The years passed, and Felicia grew to adolescence. She stumbled through common growing pains, social anxieties, and crushes on fellow students—in her case, mostly girls. Aunt Althea offered understanding and support, helping smooth the way through these uncomfortable rites of passage.

Then, when Felicia was just fourteen, everything changed once again. On an ordinary

Running along the smooth golden beach

Saturday morning, Horace showed up at the Wexhill house, looking as if he'd been badly beaten. His face was shadowed with exhaustion, his clothes torn and grubby.

Apparently he'd ventured into the treacherous and largely uncharted 'Far Realm' searching for a powerful artifact. In the process he'd angered an otherworldly entity who now hunted him, bent on revenge.

Horace begged Althea for help, but within moments his pursuer appeared, manifesting in a swirl of alien magic. Great tendrils of purple and magenta energy swirled around the terrifying creature, while dark tentacles writhed on its skull-like head.

Althea tried to reason with it, but no mercy showed in the creature's hollow eyes. Lightning crackled over its bony hands, as it launched a devastating attack. Her aunt shouted for Felicia to run to the bedroom and put on the magically warded coat hanging in the closet. Those were the last words she ever spoke.

By the time Felicia obeyed, sliding her arms into the red wool sleeves of the coat, the house exploded around her. She snapped open her aunt's spell-shielded umbrella, just as the roof fell in. The umbrella protected her from major injuries but not from being knocked unconscious.

Later, when Felicia roused, the house lay demolished around her, most everything pulverized to dust. Only the charred bones of her aunt remained, with no sign of Horace.

Dark tentacles writhed on its skull-like head

He didn't show his face until several months later, claiming it was all an unfortunate accident. By that time Felicia had been packed off to boarding school, the incident described by the press as a random terrorist bombing.

Horace made no attempt to gain guardianship of Felicia—probably because her inheritance from Althea barely covered school tuition, room, and board. There was nothing in it to benefit him.

He visited the one time only, perhaps seeking absolution. Felicia proved cold and unforgiving. Whether his actions were intended or not, she held him responsible for her beloved Aunt's death. She wanted nothing more to do with him or the hidden worlds of magic.

Felicia's heart was thoroughly wrung out, her mind full of horrific images that plagued her nightmares for years. She felt utterly alone, her primary solace lying in books—the school library becoming a much needed haven.

Eventually she attended university and graduated as a credentialed librarian. After an initial placement at the Wexhill Collection, she managed to get a job in Port Lorence, her favorite seaside town. Proximity to the ocean brought her comfort, as did her new job. She settled into a routine—pleasant work, long walks on the beach, a few casual friends, as many books as she wanted to read, and annual holidays taken at the best bird watching destinations.

Felicia cultivated a life of orderly calm for the next decade. Simple and safe, that's what she wanted. No nasty surprises. No deep wells of emotion. All that was behind her now, wasn't it?

Just lately, things had felt a little off—perhaps starting with the man drowning, three cottages down the row. That tragedy served as a sharp reminder of her own mortality and raised niggling doubts about whether she was making the most of her life. If Felicia was perfectly honest, she might even admit to a growing boredom with her tidy predictable existence.

Now, here she sat, listening to The Great and Terrible's story. This brave little creature had lost so much to her uncle's ruthless pursuit of power—risking everything to venture through the Human world and find her, hoping for some form of justice. His courage and his heartbreak both touched her deeply, stirring up all sorts of difficult feelings.

With Horace dead, Felicia had hoped never to deal with her family's legacy again. The estate was sold, to pay off her uncle's monumental debts, and no close relatives remained. It had seemed she might finally be free of the past.

But how could she turn her back on The Great and Terrible? He deserved better, having suffered from Horace's actions, just as she had. Felicia could not refuse him help, even if that choice jeopardized her carefully maintained equilibrium.

CHAPTER THREE

"There are no words for how sorry I am," Felicia said. "I too lost my family when I was young." She hoped The Great and Terrible sensed her sincerity. "Nothing is ever the same again, no matter how many years pass. That loss is always part of you."

"I still have dreams about them," he murmured, swiping away a tear. "Sometimes, if I'm lucky, they're happy memories. But often I have nightmares about the day your uncle found our clanhold."

His words pierced like a blade. How well she knew such dreams. They had plagued her nights with visions of Althea facing the skull-faced monster, of her aunt's bones charred and blackened, of Felicia's inability to stop the carnage.

"I understand better than you might imagine." Her eyes pricked with unshed tears, her throat tightening with emotion. "I can't bring your parents and siblings back, but there may be something I can do about the Crown of

Visions. It's small recompense, I realize, but better than nothing."

"If you return the Crown of Visions to us, it would be a great service. My sister, The Wise and Wondrous, is suited for leadership of our clan. But the Nemurithain chieftains have always worn the Crown, since the very earliest of times, using its powers for guidance. She feels hesitant to accept the role without it."

"I can't promise anything," Felicia responded. "But I do have a hunch where the Crown might be."

"Please, tell me."

"Horace had a secret 'lair' hidden at the edge of my family's property, behind a waterfall. I suspect he kept his treasures there, away from prying eyes."

"But would it remain undisturbed now, after his death?"

"Possibly. My uncle died quite unexpectedly…violently, in fact. He was stabbed by an unknown assailant, most likely some rival sorcerer with a score to settle."

"That doesn't surprise me."

"Indeed. As far as I know, he had no close friends or partners to share his secret hoard with. When the estate sold, the buyers were of a non-magical sort. So they had no inkling what types of artifacts might be secreted around the property. There's a good chance the Crown and various other treasures might still be there. In fact, I should consider returning all the stolen artifacts to their proper owners…if that's possible."

"This is better than I hoped for." The Great and Terrible beamed at her. "You are cut from much finer cloth than your uncle."

"I should think so. He was an absolute villain." Feeling a need to move—to work out the antsy tingling in her limbs—Felicia rose and rinsed her teacup in the sink. "I can't say the whole thing doesn't make me nervous, but clearly it has to be done."

She began to pace, laying out a preliminary plan. "The library closes early today, because of the Lobster Festival this weekend. If I leave by mid-afternoon and book a sleeping compartment on the train, I can be rested by the time I reach Traitham, which is the closest town to Fisk Hall. It will be full dark by then, but that's probably best, as I will be trespassing." The thought sent an anxious shiver over her skin. "With the moon full, I should be able to see well enough to make my way upriver to the waterfall. And then..." She huffed uneasily. "Well, then I'll have to see if my sorcery breaking is up to the challenge of Horace's wardings. I must admit my skills are a little rusty."

"I will accompany you," The Great and Terrible stated, standing up straighter and puffing out his chest. "You may need my help."

"That's a kind offer, but you've already risked so much, just by coming to find me. It's my responsibility to do the rest. Besides, this may be a wild goose chase. I could be wrong about the location of my uncle's treasures."

"Regardless, I can't let you face such danger alone." The Great and Terrible approached and placed his tiny hand on hers. "Although I came here prepared to confront an enemy, it's clear you are nothing of the sort. We are allies in this quest, and I will defend your life as if it was my own. This I promise, on the blood of all the Brathoss warriors who have come before me."

"I'm honored, and I promise to do the same for you." She tried to match his solemn demeanor. "Although I'm not a sorcerer or a warrior, what talents I do have are at your service."

He nodded, obviously pleased. "Since we are now sworn comrades, you may call me GT. It is rather quicker to say than The Great and Terrible."

"Thank you…GT. And now we really should get some sleep. I start at the library in a few hours, and it's going to be a big day."

~*~

Felicia woke with the bedding tangled around her legs. Apparently she'd thrashed in her sleep, harrowed by the same nightmare she'd had so many times before. It wasn't surprising, considering the conversation with GT before bed. All the old traumas were unavoidably stirred up.

Residual adrenaline made her feel both jittery and tired, as she shuffled to the bathroom. The mirror showed her reflection pinched and pale from the restless night. Felicia's eyes—usually her most attractive feature—looked like burnt raisins in uncooked dough. Ugh! Nothing to do but splash cold water on her face, drink some strong tea, and make the best of it.

The morning dawned crisp and cool, with a brisk breeze blowing off the sea. Felicia loved this time of year, with the first hint of autumn sharpening the air. She wore her russet-colored cardigan with the large front pockets, sufficient in size to carry GT, who insisted on going to work with her. The yarn matched well enough with his fur for camouflage, and the looser knit allowed him to peer through the tiny gaps.

"When I arrived last night," he told her, "I saw a suspicious fellow lurking across the street. You may be in more peril than you realize."

"This neighborhood is full of suspicious looking fellows," she countered. "I can't imagine why anyone would spy on me. Besides, you'd be much more comfortable and safe staying here at the cottage."

"No. I'll go along today and keep my eyes open. You may need me, and it's wise to be prepared for the worst."

In clear weather Felicia usually walked to work, appreciating a vigorous stretch of the legs. But knowing what the coming night held, she thought it best to conserve energy and take the tram.

Riding through town, she felt an uncomfortable prickling on the back of her neck, as if someone was indeed watching her. Could GT have been correct, or had his warning words simply triggered her imagination? She glanced around, noticing nothing odd about the other passengers.

It was probably just nerves. She focused out the window, watching the morning pedestrians. Everything would be fine. She just needed to remain calm and take this day one step at time.

Once at the library, things proceeded normally, until she spotted an individual leaning against the wall, hands in his pockets, staring at her. At least she thought he was staring at her. Truth was, a custom-made gas mask obscured any view of his face. He might have been dozing, for all she knew.

After a series of terrorist attacks on chemical and gas facilities around the capital, a subset of the wealthy class had taken to wearing decorative gas masks as a sort of macabre accessory. They were typically made from expensive materials, often elaborately embellished, and always absurd—in Felicia's opinion. What statement were people trying to make with these morbid affectations?

The 'doomsday fashion' fad, as it was called in the press, had spread from the larger northern cities to reach even provincial towns like Port Lorence. Predictably it faded quickly—gas masks being uncomfortable to wear—so now only a few eccentrics continued the trend.

This fellow, for example, looked otherwise dapper in a trim plaid suit. The ensemble would have suited a straw boater or even a nice brown derby, instead of that ridiculous gas mask. At

There was something uncanny about the man

least this one remained relatively simple, without the excessive scrollwork and jewels featured on most.

Regardless, there was something uncanny about the man, beyond his questionable fashion sense. The way he continued to stare unsettled Felicia. A familiar coppery tickling started in her nose and the back of her throat, causing her to cough and sip from the cup of water at her desk.

She knew that metallic itching sensation all too well. Magic. It wasn't strong enough to glean anything specific about the purpose, but the presence of sorcery was unmistakable.

"I think I've had about enough of this," she muttered, preparing to rise and confront the stranger with her most stern librarian manner. But when she looked up, he was gone. Only a faint trace of magic lingered in the air.

By one o'clock Felicia was glad to close the library and head home. Of course the night ahead remained full of unpleasant potential, but she wouldn't dwell on it.

"One step at time," she kept reminding herself. "Just do the next thing and then the next after that."

In this case, the next thing was sharing a late lunch with GT, who no longer held her hospitality suspect. He did, however, have much to say on the subject of the masked man.

"He was up to no good, I tell you. I could sense it from across the room." GT's orange fur bristled. "We'll have trouble before this is all through. Mark my words. There will be trouble."

Felicia sighed, feeling another headache coming on. She fetched an aspirin from the bathroom and took it with a shot of whiskey in her tea. Dire times called for dire measures.

"We should travel well-armed tonight," GT continued. "I have this spear and the three throwing daggers in my belt. Also, I can breathe fire should the need arise."

"Ah...good." Felicia tried to smile encouragingly, as she imagined GT scorching the ankles of a would-be attacker.

"What about your weapons?" he asked.

"I don't own anything more lethal than a kitchen knife. But I will bring my aunt's enchanted coat and umbrella. They're bound to be helpful."

As well as providing a powerful shield, the umbrella had offensive capabilities, projecting pulses of energy to stun an opponent. The warded coat was a true wonder. In addition to its overall protective properties, it kept the wearer perfectly comfortable, never too hot or too cold, regardless of the weather. It also included a magical pocket that could hold limitless quantities without gaining in size or weight—a handy attribute on an outing such as this.

All three Fisk siblings had been given a set of these coats and umbrellas by their parents, red for Althea, blue for Ambrose, and yellow for Horace. Felicia didn't know what became of the others, but she'd cared for her aunt's like the greatest of treasures. They were her only personal mementos of Althea, everything else having been destroyed in the otherworldly attack.

After finishing her meal Felicia dressed for the night's adventure. She put on a lightweight turtleneck, sturdy trousers, and an excellent pair of hiking boots. They'd cost a pretty penny but were well worth the expense, especially when traversing difficult terrain. While the ensemble looked far from fashionable, practicality must be the priority. Besides she'd be covering it all with the spiffy red coat.

The journey by train proved uneventful, except for a brief time in the station when Felicia felt that uneasy sensation of being watched. Upon disembarking at Traitham, she looked around carefully, making sure no one followed as she left town and walked toward the estate.

The full moon shone bright enough to light Felicia's way, shimmering silver over the rippling river. She hurried along, with GT sitting alert, holding onto her coat's shoulder strap. Trilling calls of night birds carried through the darkness between trees, and once a pair of river otters startled at her passing, slipping down the bank like two sleek shadows.

Eventually, as the moon sank westward, Felicia heard a familiar roar and knew the falls lay ahead. Rounding the final bend, she took a shaky breath, her heart beginning to race. There it was, the river hurling itself down twenty feet, in a rushing blur of sound and spray. Fine mist wrapped the falls like a white veil, lit by the moon. The sight was beautiful, if also rather

Fine mist wrapped the falls like a white veil

daunting. Was she really going to walk through that mass of pounding water?

Felicia hopped gingerly along the path of wet boulders, grateful for her hiking boots with their superb tread. Water droplets clung to her hair and eyelashes, beading on the red wool of her coat.

"Well, this is it," she said, opening the red umbrella. "Let's hope for the best."

CHAPTER FOUR

Stepping under the waterfall took courage, but not as much as facing her uncle's wardings. While water beat down over the sides of Felicia's umbrella, she felt the increasing pressure of Horace's magic assaulting her senses. With each step forward, the sorcery pushed back, hounding her with stabbing pain, vertigo, nausea, and confusion. She couldn't concentrate enough for an attempt at breaking the spell. To make matters worse, there was a very real danger of losing her balance and falling on the slick rocks.

"You can do this!" GT shouted to be heard over the thundering torrent. "Don't let him best you!"

"I have to retreat a little. This is all too much. I can't think straight."

Felicia stepped back to the edge of the falling sheet of water. Here, she could still sense Horace's wardings, but their effect lessened.

"Don't give up," GT encouraged. "We're so close!"

"I'm not giving up. I just need some space to focus."

Her aunt's coat and umbrella shielded against physical dangers like lightning, jets of flame, or poison darts. Some wardings employed such devices, but her uncle's were more subtle. He'd crafted them with his talent for illusion and mind control, and so they altered a person's perception. The pain and dizziness felt all too real, but there was no actual substance to them.

With a straightforward path and easy footing, she might have risked pushing through, trying to ignore the warding's effects. But here, in this deluge of water and sharp rocks, that option was far too hazardous. She needed her senses clear.

"Horace's magic is unusually complex," she told GT. "There are too many different elements, and the lines of the spell are so tightly woven, I can't find a way to pick them apart."

"What can we do?"

"Give me a minute. Maybe I can find a loose thread somewhere, if I look close enough."

Calling up Aunt Althea's training, Felicia closed her eyes and steadied her breath. She pushed away all distractions and concentrated solely on Horace's spell. It appeared to glow in the darkness behind her eyelids, intricate circles of pulsing energy, bound with myriad symbols. The idea of dismantling it seemed impossible, but that might be part of its intended effect, overwhelming anyone who tried to break the warding.

"There has to be a way," she muttered, remembering how arrogant and careless her uncle had been in life. He assumed his own superiority and so underestimated the abilities of others. What if the seeming perfection of this spell was nothing but an illusion, crafted to cover its flaws?

With that encouraging thought, Felicia willed the spell to turn in her mind, studying each small area, ignoring the distracting glamor of color and light. After what felt like an eternity, she spotted a loose thread.

"Got it!" she crowed, plucking the strand of magic and following it to the heart of the spell, unraveling as she went. Within a few minutes, the whole warding began to break down, eventually falling away like ash in a strong wind.

Felicia's entire being tingled with the exertion of using her talent. It felt good, like running fast across an open field, after too many years plodding through a swamp. This was what she was born to do!

That thought, and the exhilaration following it, surprised her. Had she been mistaken, turning her back on all things magical? Perhaps there were positives to be found in her hidden ability. Accessing it again certainly felt right.

Still a little giddy from her victory, Felicia passed under the waterfall and into the darkness beyond.

"Luminn," she called out, guessing that Horace would have glow globes installed in his

The whole warding began to break down

secret lair. Such magical mechanisms were handy, requiring nothing but a word to activate. Even someone as spell-impaired as Felicia could work them.

Floating circles of colored light flared at her command. Red, blue, purple, and green, illuminated the way along a short passage and into a low oblong chamber. The place was a mess, with books and papers piled haphazardly on the minimal furniture. Jars, pouches, wooden boxes, and random arcane paraphernalia scattered the floor, with no seeming logic to their placement.

Such disorganization irritated Felicia like the whine of mosquitoes or the crackle of radio static. How could anyone function with such chaos around them?

"It could take a while to find the Crown in all this," GT observed. "Where do we begin?"

"Good question." Felicia looked around with distaste. Sorting through her uncle's clutter felt only slightly more appealing than getting her toes chewed by hungry eels. But it must be done.

"Why don't you start here by the entryway," she suggested, setting GT carefully on the floor. "I'll take the far end of the room, and we can meet in the middle."

Shaking off her reluctance, Felicia dove in, starting with one pile before moving on to the next and the next. To her surprise most of the hoard was rubbish. Horace must have been quite a magpie, collecting every trinket that caught his eye. He also wrote reams of bad poetry and self-aggrandizing journal entries.

Thankfully, within the first hour, Felicia found a useful item—a list of her uncle's most prized treasures, including where and how he'd obtained them. Apparently he took pride in his swindling and thieving, considering both a sign of uncommon cleverness.

Shortly after that GT discovered an exquisite crystal rod, in which Felicia sensed significant power. She looked on Horace's list and verified the item was called the Prism Wand. It rightfully belonged to the Aldrahen—inhabitants of the Dark Realm, like the Brathoss and Nyarra.

"I'll need to return this, after we take the Crown of Visions back to your people." Felicia turned the delicate crystal in her hands, marveling at the sparkling rainbow of light within. "What purpose do you suppose the Aldrahen used it for? Aren't they exceptional artists and architects? I remember reading about their city, Ellethon, one of the great wonders of the Dark Realm."

"I suppose." GT seemed less than enthusiastic. "We Brathoss don't have many dealings with the Aldrahen. They're a stuck up bunch and can't be trusted to keep their word. You'd do well to steer clear of them."

"But I must try to return this wand. My uncle wrote here that it's one of their ruling family's most valued heirlooms. I can't just keep it."

"Well, you'd best have me along when you go to Ellethon. I'll keep an eye out for trouble, so you don't get hoodwinked by those Aldrahen Mages."

"Thank you. That's a generous offer. I don't know anything about the Dark Realm, except what I read in Widdershin's field guide. Mind you, I had that practically memorized. It was a favorite of mine, partly because of the beautiful illustrations."

"Is it that book there?" GT pointed to the top of a pile he'd already searched. "I glanced through a few pictures. They do a fair job showing what it's like, though, in my opinion, the artist makes everything too pretty. The Dark Realm isn't a romantic fairyland full of glowing creatures and twinkly lights."

"But isn't there a variety of flora and fauna, most with bioluminescence of one sort of another?"

"Oh yes. There's many a sight that'll take your breath away. But the flora is mostly poisonous, and the fauna will just as likely eat you for lunch. It's not a place for the faint of heart."

"Duly noted."

Felicia picked up the book to find it was *Denizens of the Dark: A Field Guide* by Thomas Widdershins. Indeed, this was a limited edition, with full-color illustrations, exactly like the copy Aunt Althea had given her for her thirteenth birthday.

Denizens of the Dark had been printed by a sorcery-friendly publishing house that made a decent profit from the hidden community of magic users. This field guide was considered the best source for information on any secret realm, as the author spent months exploring, relating accurate hands-on experience rather than the hearsay that filled most such books. Felicia used to pour over it as a girl, fascinated by the many different creatures, cultures, and regions described.

Holding a copy now brought back memories of lazy afternoons spent reading under her aunt's old maple tree—or evenings curled on the sofa, while rain pattered outside, and a cozy fire crackled on the hearth. She'd read especially interesting sections aloud to Althea, while their gray cat, Longshanks, purred on the cushions next to her.

Felicia's hands shook as she opened the cover, some intuition warning her of what she'd find. Sure enough, there was her aunt's precise penmanship, just as she remembered it.

To my beloved niece, on her thirteenth birthday. May this open a world of wonder for you. Love, Althea

Her mind reeled. How did Horace get his hands on this particular copy? When had he stolen it?

An image flashed into Felicia's mind, of that terrible Saturday morning when she was fourteen. This book had been laying on the side table closest the door. Horace must have spotted it, when he came in. Perhaps he was

Memories of lazy afternoons spent reading

already planning a treasure hunt in the Dark Realm.

The shock hit Felicia like a physical blow. It hurt more than she could have imagined, to see her aunt's handwriting, still so familiar after all these years—and to realize Horace stole this book before abandoning his sister to her death. He'd certainly had his wits about him, enough to spot a useful item and pocket it. His claims of having been in a panic, of having fled without thought, were false.

It was too much. Felicia's steely self-control buckled, as tears came unbidden. Grief and anger mingled, pouring out of her. She couldn't fight them back this time, sobs wracking her body, as long-buried pain surged to the surface.

"He knew exactly what he was doing!" she gasped. "He led that monster to our house, so Althea could distract it. And then he ran. The filthy, lying bastard!"

Felicia buckled over, face pressed to her knees, shuddering and weeping. She wanted so badly to see her aunt again, to hear her voice, and give her a hug. She also wanted to rip her uncle to shreds, tear him limb from limb and stomp on the pieces.

GT climbed to her shoulder and stood there gently patting her cheek. Small though he was, his presence helped. Here was someone who understood what she'd gone through, because he had faced similar loss.

Finally the tears ran dry. Felicia sat upright, feeling hollowed out, yet somehow clearer. She'd needed to let loose like that for a very long time.

"I can continue the search alone," GT said kindly, "if the process is too painful for you."

"No. I'm more determined than ever to return items to their rightful owners...starting with this." Felicia slipped *Denizens of the Dark: A Field Guide* into the pocket of her coat.

She searched with renewed vigor, using her magical sense as a guide in finding the important artifacts from Horace's list. If some of the less valuable trinkets had also been stolen, she knew of no way to track down the owners and return them. The night was waning, and she needed to focus on what could reasonably be accomplished in the time remaining.

At last GT uncovered the Crown of Visions, in amongst a pile of expeditionary gear: grappling hooks, rope, bedroll, tinder box, travel-sized glow globes and such. He called to Felicia, holding the Crown aloft like a trophy, beaming.

"Isn't it beautiful!" He placed the treasure in her hand so she could take a closer look. The Crown was about the size of a large man's thumb ring, made from an uncommonly dark wood. The magic within it felt ancient, rich, and deep.

"Is this ebony?" she asked, admiring the natural smooth finish and spiraling whirls of the wood grain.

"The Crown is made from a piece of the Oracle Tree." GT told her. "That's where the power comes from for visions of the past, the future, and places far away."

"A useful item."

"But our chieftains can't command visions from the Crown, any more than pilgrims who visit the Oracle Tree can direct what they receive. Visions are given with a wisdom beyond our understanding. We must accept them gratefully, whatever they may be."

"Interesting. I remember reading about the Oracle Tree in Widdershin's field guide. He claimed there were no artifacts made from its wood, because the Tree would not allow even a twig to be taken."

GT nodded. "There's not another like our Crown in all the realms. If a person tries to cut or break a piece off the Tree, they're struck senseless by its magic."

"Then how does this exist?" Felicia handed him back the Crown of Visions.

"Long ago our very first chieftan, The Mighty and Brilliant Sorbahnlimah Nemurithain Brathoss, burrowed down among the roots of the young Oracle Tree. Once there, she sang a song so beautiful and powerful, the Tree offered up a piece of its heart to her. It is the ultimate pride and legacy of our clan."

"What a wonderful story!" exclaimed Felicia. "I'm so glad The Crown will finally be back where it belongs. Would you like to carry it, or shall I put it in my pocket with all the rest?"

"Since your coat is warded, best to keep it there with the other treasures. We could still

The Tree offered up a piece of its heart

meet with trouble tonight, and I would hate to lose the Crown a second time."

"Very well." She slid it down into the endless pocket, along with Horace's expeditionary gear. Such things might come in handy traveling through the Dark Realm.

Felicia had no idea how she'd return items to the more remote and challenging locations, such as the Far Realm and the Elemental Realm. But that was a problem for another day. *First things first*, as Aunt Althea always said.

After one more sweep of the chamber, she felt confident of having found most of the powerful artifacts. A few items on Horace's list remained unaccounted for, but that couldn't be helped. She had done her best. It was time to leave.

CHAPTER FIVE

Stepping out from under the waterfall, Felicia saw the moon was down, and only stars remained to light her way. Fortunately, she'd taken Horace's small transportable glow globes. She rested her hand at the top of her coat pocket and visualized one of them. In an instant the item materialized, cupped in her palm.

That was a marvelous feature of Althea's coat. Not only did the pocket hold limitless quantities, but the wearer could call up any specific item they wished, with merely a thought.

"Luminn," she commanded, and the small golf-ball-sized globe shone rosy pink.

Felicia held it up, casting a circle of light several feet in diameter. She picked her way over the wet boulders to shore, and set out briskly along the riverbank towards Traitham. GT sat on her shoulder, humming happily to himself.

How satisfying, to have retrieved the Crown of Visions, and all the other precious artifacts. Felicia smiled to herself. She looked forward to arriving home and having a nice hot cup of tea, before going to sleep in her own comfortable bed. Thank goodness she didn't have to work until Monday.

Suddenly three figures stepped out of the forest on her left. The middle fellow was big, over six feet tall, with shoulders like an ox. He wore a belted trench coat and a fedora pulled low over his brow. The other two individuals were harder to see, holding back in the shadows of the trees.

"I'll just take whatever you found in Fisk's cave," the large man said, his voice thick and oily. Felicia sensed sorcery hovering in the air around him.

"The only thing I found is this glow globe," she lied, tossing the light onto the ground between them. "The place has been ransacked already. It was a complete waste of time." Thankfully, her coat lay smoothly, giving no indication of the treasure trove hidden inside the magic pocket.

"Lady, you don't want to mess with me and the boys. We can bust you up good, if you don't play along. Now give us the loot!"

"I don't think so." Felicia gripped Althea's umbrella, reminding herself of the command to activate its stun function. This would be the first time she'd used it.

"I guess we're going to have to do this the hard way," the thug growled, proving himself appallingly short on imagination.

He stepped forward, rolling his shoulders and muttering a string of arcane phrases.

Monstrous pincers burst from his right arm. They looked like a cross between crab, spider, and something otherworldly.

His left arm began to bulge, ready to reveal its own uncanny armory. If this display was meant to intimidate, Felicia had to acknowledge its effectiveness. She was now well and truly frightened.

The man lunged at her, pincers waving. Felicia raised her umbrella and shouted the command for stun. A pulse of energy shot out, dropping the thug in his tracks. At the same time the recoil knocked Felicia backwards. She stumbled and fell hard with the wind knocked out of her.

Several things happened at once. The two other men ran forward, while GT charged to meet them, bellowing a surprisingly loud battle cry. Meanwhile, a fourth individual appeared out of the river, racing to engage the remaining thugs.

Still dazed, Felicia couldn't make sense of what she saw. Were those fish scales on the fourth figure, reflecting iridescent in the glow globe's light. Had GT just set a man's trousers on fire?

She struggled to her feet, swinging the umbrella, unsure where to aim. By that time, she needn't have bothered. Both thugs fell to the ground, one knocked out by the mysterious aquatic figure—the other rolling and smacking at his smoldering pants. He soon fell unconscious, as GT leapt onto his chest and

Monstrous pincers burst from his right arm

expertly applied pressure to a point on the man's neck, using the butt end of his small but sturdy spear.

The sleek scaled individual stepped into the light and met Felicia's gaze. The woman was clearly Nyarran and unexpectedly familiar. Though obviously no longer a child—time and maturity having worked many changes upon her—certain features remained recognizable. The shape of her beautiful golden eyes was one, as well as the angle of her cheekbones. If there remained any doubt, the scar running across her left eyebrow proved it. This really was her!

"Islen?" Felicia moved closer, feeling as though she floated in a dream. Could the night get any more fantastical?

"I hope you're glad to see me." Islen spoke hesitantly, appearing ready to flee at any moment.

"Of course I'm glad to see you." Felicia couldn't help grinning like a fool. "I'm thrilled! And I would really, really like to hug you."

"Oh...yes. I'd like that too." Islen's lips quirked into a smile, revealing that little dimple at the corner of her mouth, which Felicia remembered so fondly.

The two women embraced, and the years seemed to fall away. They stood outside time and space, two kindred spirits reunited.

"I just can't believe it's you," Felicia said, wiping at the tears sliding down her cheeks. "It's like a...a miracle."

"I'm relieved you feel that way." Islen laughed, shaking her head. "Everyone warned me not to seek you out. They said Humans change as adults, no longer believing in magic or other worlds. They become dangerous and hostile toward the unknown…toward anything they see as a threat."

"I'm glad that didn't stop you finding me." Felicia paused, stunned by the wonder of it all. "How did you find me?"

"I never completely gave up looking. After that final time we met, when you told me your parents had died, I kept coming here, hoping I'd see you. But you disappeared completely."

"I'm sorry, Islen. Aunt Althea took me to her home in Wexhill. She had a big fight with my uncle, over the will, and we left in rush. There was never a chance to meet with you again."

"I understand." Islen rested her hand reassuringly on Felicia's arm. "That must have been a horrible time in your life. I remember worrying about what might have happened to you…so much so, I made a pilgrimage to the Oracle Tree, hoping it would show me if you were safe and well."

"But that's such a difficult journey!"

Islen grinned. "You know me. I love a challenge."

"What did the tree show you?"

"I received a vision of you as an adult, reading a bedtime story to a little boy. It let me know you would survive and find a place in the world. So, I felt more at peace with our parting. Still, I always kept my eyes and ears open as I explored. Over the years, I went all the way to the northern glaciers, south to the equator, and east as far as the hundred islands. And I never gave up hope of seeing you again."

"So, you happened upon me tonight by chance?"

"Not exactly. Two days ago, I was swimming along the tidewater near Port Lorence. It was late dusk, and I heard someone reading aloud. The window was open, and I stopped under the deck of the cottage, where it overhangs the river. I recognized the story you were reading, and your voice. It was exactly like my vision from the Oracle Tree. I couldn't believe my luck."

"But you didn't make yourself known? Why?"

"At first I meant to, but then I doubted if you'd be happy to see me. You're a mother now, and probably married…living with people who'll see me as a monster. I didn't want to disrupt your life, and I wondered if you'd maybe forgotten our friendship."

"I'm not married or a mother. That boy is a neighbor's son, who I take care of once in a while. But regardless of all that, I could never forget you, Islen. You were the dearest friend of my childhood. I treasure the memories of our time together."

"I feel the same way," Islen responded. "I just let fear hold me back from speaking to you."

"But you came here, tonight."

"Yes. I had to make sure you were safe. The Oracle Tree gave me that particular vision for a reason. The timing of finding you seems important, especially with the arrival of the Brathoss warrior yesterday." Here she nodded at GT, who still stood on the unconscious thug's chest. "I noticed strange folk watching your house, and it worried me."

"Ha! I told you," GT said. "Someone's been waiting for you to go after your uncle's hoard."

"Was that you I saw in the river last night," Felicia asked Islen, "when I went out on the deck?"

"It was. I stayed and listened to your conversation. As soon as you went to bed, I began traveling here, so I'd be in place and ready if you needed help."

"I'm grateful for it." Felicia reached out and took Islen's hand in her own. "You've been a better friend to me than I could have imagined."

"I hate to cut short this reunion," GT said, "but we'd best get gone before these fellows revive. I don't fancy another fight."

"He's right," Islen agreed. "And we should cover our trail."

"How do you propose we do that?" Felicia asked, feeling more than a little inadequate for the challenges ahead. Did she really intend to travel through the Dark Realm and beyond? A career in library science seemed poor preparation for such a venture.

"This side of the river has your tracks going to and from the falls," Islen explained. "If we step carefully along that trail, it would take an expert tracker to distinguish the new marks. Then we cross the river using the boulders just below the falls, where the water washes away any trace. On the far bank, we drag a tree limb behind, as we go, making sure to obscure any evidence of our passing. Another two miles upriver, I know of a fishing boat, tucked into the shore, which you can use to cross back to this side, while I swim. After that, we probably won't need to be as careful. The trail will be cold and confusing for anyone who's looking."

"Well, that's a very thorough plan. And I'm grateful you'll be coming with us. Your help tonight has already been invaluable. I just have one question. Why are we going upstream? Shouldn't I be headed back to the train station in Traitham?"

"If you want to do exactly what these villains expect," GT said. "There may be others waiting for you, in case the first three failed."

"Oh. I hadn't thought of that. But how am I to get home?"

"You probably shouldn't go home," Islen warned. "That's the first place they'll look. Better to leave for the Dark Realm now. At least then you can return the Crown of Visions to the Nemurithain clanhold, before your pursuers have a chance to catch up."

"There's another item to return as well, a wand for the Aldrehen."

"All the more reason for speed." Islen spoke with urgency. "The sooner you get these treasures out of your hands the better."

"But I haven't prepared for a journey!"

"You already have the expedition gear from your uncle's lair," GT reminded her. "And that coat will keep you comfortable, no matter where we go."

"A change of clothes might be nice," Felicia grumbled. "But I suppose it's not technically necessary. I will need provisions though. And I've got to inform someone at the library that I won't be in for work Monday."

"There's a village, a few miles west of here," Islen said. "It's not much out of our way, heading toward the closest entrance to the Dark Realm. You can purchase supplies there. But you won't need much. We can reach my home the day after tomorrow, and I'll provide anything else you need."

"You live that close?" Felicia felt a stab of shame at her own lack of initiative. "You mean I could have come and found you that easily, at any time?"

"There's nothing easy about it," Islen countered. "First you need to know where a Dark Realm entrance is. Then you need the magic keywords to open the door. Beyond that, you'd have to navigate a dangerous, alien realm without any idea how to find my home. There's no use in regrets. Just focus on what to do now."

"And what we need to do is leave!" GT insisted.

"Very well," Felicia surrendered. "Let's go."

~*~

The three traveled upriver until dawn, at which point they turned west toward a range of wooded hills. When they neared a small village, Islen left in order to stay hidden. She planned to skirt around the Human habitation and meet her companions further on.

Felicia visited the grocers for food and the post office to send a telegram. It informed her library supervisor that a family emergency had come up, and she wouldn't be in to work all week.

A safe distance beyond the village, Islen rejoined Felicia and GT. She led them to a spot she'd found to rest. The small clearing sat well off the beaten path, screened on all sides by dense trees and brush.

Islen and GT offered to trade at keeping watch, while Felicia slept. She began by insisting on taking a turn, but exhaustion prevailed. As soon as she lay down on the sun-warmed grass, her body surrendered. She slept deep and hard, barely moving a muscle for several hours.

In the late afternoon, Islen woke her, saying it was time they move on. Felicia shared out some of the food she'd bought, and they trekked deeper into the hills.

At first the going was tough. Felicia felt stiff and sore from sleeping on the ground, though Islen and GT seemed none the worse for wear—both of them used to the rigors of adventuring. In fact, the two had hit it off rather well. As the group climbed higher, through increasingly rugged terrain, Islen and GT chatted happily, sharing what could only be called Dark Realm gossip.

Felicia listened with interest. Their conversation brought back more of *The*

Denizens of the Dark content to her mind—those memories still intact, requiring only gentle prodding to surface.

As the surrounding country grew wilder and more majestic—Felicia's reluctance transformed to excitement. Yes, the way ahead was daunting. But what an opportunity! She was about to enter the Dark Realm, to see firsthand those wonders so long imagined. Surely an undertaking such as this was worth a few sore muscles.

The sun set in amber-rose glory, and dusk gradually descended. A thin mist formed, softening the edges of the world around them. The group entered a narrow valley between high ridges, coming within sight of a massive tree. It towered above any neighbors, the leaves deep red, when other foliage had barely begun to turn.

The closer they drew, the more monumental it appeared. Especially when it became clear the tree actually grew from the bottom of a deep ravine. Until now, they'd only seen the top two thirds.

As Felicia stood at the edge of the ravine looking down, she could barely make out the base of the trunk, far below in the mist and shadows. A faint trail cut switchbacks down the worryingly steep slope, more suited for mountain goats than people.

"You're sure this is the place?" Felicia asked. She wouldn't mind a bit if it wasn't. That descent looked perilous.

It towered above any neighbors

"I'm sure," Islen answered. "This isn't the usual way I go but will work well enough. We should hurry, before it gets full dark."

"I am *not* hurrying down that trail," Felicia countered, "and neither should you. The last thing we need is one of us to break our leg...or neck. A glow globe will suffice when the last evening light is gone."

"You might want your hands free," GT suggested. "Looks to me like we'll be rock climbing part of the way."

"I'll hold the glow globe in my teeth if I have to. But I will not *hurry*. Hastiness leads to carelessness, which only ends up taking more time. That's what my Aunt Althea always said, and she was a very smart woman."

Islen and GT exchanged a humorous look, which Felicia did not miss.

"All right, you two. I may not be the most intrepid adventurer, but I'm doing my best. You'll just have to bear with me."

"You're doing very well," GT said, giving her shoulder a comforting pat. "We know you're not used to this sort of thing."

The descent into the ravine seemed to take forever. Felicia did end up needing both hands, in order to keep from sliding down the near-vertical sides. She did not, however, have to resort to holding a glow globe in her teeth. Islen, who was much more agile, managed the climb down with only one hand, using the other to hold their light.

At last they reached the bottom and stood in front of a giant tangle of tree roots. The trunk stretched above them, up and up, till it became only a vague dark shape against the indigo sky.

"What now?" Felicia wondered, studying the coiled roots, some as wide around as wagon wheels.

"I'll try the opening incantation and hope it works," Islen responded. "A few entrances have different phrases, and they do get changed from time to time. But I know several, so we should be fine."

As predicted, after she recited two incantations that accomplished nothing, the third awakened an arch of glowing blue sigils in the tree trunk. Just below them, a doorway opened. It stood approximately five feet high by two feet wide—just large enough for an adult Human to squeeze through.

The group climbed over tree roots to the trunk where the doorway stood. Felicia held out a glow globe and peered inside. Cramped stairs spiraled down into the darkness. It was impossible to see how far they went.

"Oh dear," she muttered to herself. "This is not going to be fun."

CHAPTER SIX

If climbing into the ravine had been arduous, then entering the Dark Realm felt doubly so. The stairs wound on and on, steep and narrow, never changing except to go from wood to stone. Felicia hunched forward, her head brushing the ceiling, her feet seeming too big for the small steps. She refrained from complaining, however, as Islen was even taller than her and managed the stairs without issue.

By the time they reached the bottom, Felicia was done in. She gazed wearily around at the dim lifeless cavern they'd entered, feeling decidedly underwhelmed by the scenery. Where were the giant candelabra mushrooms and the fluttering glimmerweirs? Where were the chrysolite groves and leaping golden spireels? Not a single thing moved or grew in this expanse of gray rock.

"I need to eat and rest before we continue," she told the others. "My legs are wobbly."

Islen nodded. "It looks safe enough for now, but we shouldn't stay long. Entrances attract those who prey on travelers. We need to find a more sheltered spot, before stopping to sleep."

After a brief respite, they started out once more. Thankfully a clear path led through the cavern, relatively flat and easy to traverse. Distance was difficult to gauge in such monotonous surroundings, but they seemed to walk at least a mile before nearing the far end. Here the air felt warmer, holding a taint of sulfur and smoke.

"There may have been an eruption nearby," Islen warned. "We should be careful."

Widdershin's field guide warned about the geologic instability in the Dark Realm. Earthquakes were relatively common, as were small-scale volcanic eruptions. Cracks and fissures sometimes appeared, allowing magma to seep out, or deep vents expelled bursts of boiling water.

Indeed, the next cavern they entered was hazy with smoke. Sparks of ash drifted in the air. Whatever plants or fungi had grown there were now blackened and smoldering, giving the place a hellish appearance.

Felicia held a handkerchief in front of her nose and mouth, offering one to Islen for the same purpose. GT assured her he was fine. Brathoss didn't mind a bit of fire and smoke. Indeed, they found it invigorating.

About halfway through the cavern, Felicia spotted a flock of black birds perched on the scorched remains of something large and tree like—perhaps a gigantic antler fungus. The birds appeared slightly smaller than crows, but

Their eyes glowed bright as embers

with only one leg apiece, centered beneath each sleek dark body. Even more unsettling, their eyes glowed bright as embers.

"Blasted orvits!" GT cursed. "Those beaks can shred flesh in a matter of seconds. My grandfather lost his life to a flock of them."

"They might not risk attacking the three of us," Islen said, slowing her pace and studying the flock warily. The birds watched the travelers with keen interest, fixing them in the stare of countless burning eyes.

"I know a possible distraction," Felicia offered, remembering a section of *Denizens of the Dark* recounting Widdershin's experience with orvits. "They're supposed to like shiny things."

She fished a handful of coins out of her trouser pocket and threw them as hard as she could. The coins caught what little light shone in the cavern—dull and reddish though it was—sparkling as they spun through the air. The flock immediately took off, racing to the spot where the coins fell, fighting over them in a noisy squabble. Felicia and Islen sprinted away, GT holding on tight to the red coat's shoulder strap.

Once they were safely out of the fiery cavern, Felicia doubled over coughing and gasping for air. Her lungs felt as if they'd been scoured with steel wool, and her nose ran like a leaky faucet.

"We need to stop soon," she insisted between coughs. "I can't keep going much longer...not without a real rest."

"We should be able to find a suitable spot around here," Islen responded. "And I think I remember a stream up ahead."

"Oh good!" Felicia could hardly wait to rinse her raw throat and wash the gritty ash from her face.

Finally able to breathe more easily, she straightened up and looked around. The space they stood in was so large it barely seemed like an underground cavern. The roof soared high overhead, and the walls stretched away into the far distance.

All manner of oversized fungi thrived here, from massive mushrooms to puffballs as big as beach balls. There were monumental toadstools, stinkhorns, and translucent jellies. Many displayed bioluminescence in a wide array of colors, lighting the space with a rainbow glow.

Most impressive were the antler fungi, which grew to staggering proportions, some as tall as forty feet. They resembled trees just enough to create the feeling of a bizarre woodland, a landscape you might find in an opium-induced dream.

This was the Dark Realm Felicia had long wished to see, immense, alien, and strangely glorious. Exhausted though she was, a sense of awe filled her. The universe was indeed an astounding place.

~*~

After a few hours sleep, Felicia felt sufficiently restored to continue the journey. The route to Islen's home took them through more enormous caverns, filled with an ever-increasing variety of life.

In addition to myriad fungi, Felicia identified swarms of flying filligers, with narrow bodies and shimmering wings similar to dragonflies. She spotted amphibious norbols, like florescent rubbery-skinned hamsters, lounging by the edges of shallow pools. Once, she even caught a glimpse of golden spireels, tail plumes waving as they raced around a tumble of boulders.

Fan trees became more common the farther the travelers walked. These were like carnivorous plants crossed with corals, only huge. The 'trunk' and 'branches' were formed from hardened minerals, secreted by the organisms within. The 'foliage' was a colony of feathery stinging cells, primed to stun any prey that might fly or crawl too close. They grew in a variety of colors, lending a delicate if uncanny beauty to the surroundings.

A highlight of the day's trek was seeing a band of Ruskur pass by. These short stout miners may have given rise to the dwarves featured in Human fairy tales, just as Aldrahen may have led to stories of elves. Traffic between the Dark Realm and the Human world used to be more frequent, so it was hardly surprising folklore had sprung up around it.

The Ruskur band barely acknowledged Felicia, Islen, and GT. The leader raised a hand briefly in greeting, but the group trudged on undeterred. Great shaggy manes covered most of their heads and faces, revealing only brief glimpses of stony gray skin and jewel-like eyes. They bore astonishingly large loads: bags of ore, tools, weapons, and other supplies. It appeared that each individual carried more than their own weight in gear, proving what sturdy folk they were.

Finally, just as Felicia's limbs began to tremble with fatigue, Islen pointed out her home up ahead. The far wall was threaded with waterfalls. They fell in frothy steps down to the cavern floor, there merging into a small river that wound through groves of purple fan trees and the cabins of a Nyarran settlement.

Islen's home sat partway up the cavern wall, perched precariously over the rushing falls. Even from this distance Felicia could tell it was very small and rickety. The porch hung slightly askew, and the roof appeared in need of patching.

"I don't spend much time in any one place," Islen explained. "The cabin is mostly just to keep my stuff in. I only sleep a few nights here, now and then, when I want to visit my family. So it never seemed worth fixing up." She sounded embarrassed.

"I think it's very picturesque," Felicia assured her.

As they drew closer, several Nyarran individuals approached from the cabins along the river. Though the color of their eyes and scale patterns varied, they shared a certain familial resemblance with Islen. All were lean and angular, with pronounced cheekbones and pointy chins. The older Nyarra had streaks of

Perched precariously over rushing falls

yellow in the water-weed green of their hair, while the small children had yet to grow scales.

Islen's family greeted her joyfully with hugs and kisses. They also welcomed GT warmly, as Brathoss were well thought of among the Nyarra. The response to Felicia was less enthusiastic, tempered by their deep distrust of Humans. They showed her a cool kind of courtesy, edged with caution—as if she was a potentially poisonous snake invited into their midst.

Regardless of this—once they heard Islen's plan to accompany Felicia on her mission—the Nyarra offered an abundance of provisions and advice. They also provided a delicious meal in a large communal hall at the center of the settlement.

Stomach full and magical coat pocket loaded with supplies, Felicia followed Islen up the steep trail to her cabin. Despite its shabby outward appearance, the inside proved surprisingly comfortable. Cushioned furniture, handcrafted wall hangings, and a colorful rug made the place feel welcoming. Shelves displayed items brought home from Islen's many explorations—a diverse collection, ranging from exotic shells, to geodes, fossils, and more.

There was only one bed in the single-room dwelling, but it looked large enough for the women to share. GT fixed himself a little nest in a soup bowl, using a folded scarf as mattress, pillow, and blanket. Within minutes all three weary travelers fell asleep, lulled by the sounds of the waterfall.

A few hours later Felicia fell prey to the old familiar nightmare. She was fourteen again, sitting on the sofa in her aunt's Wexhill house. A sickening dread twisted her stomach as a knock sounded at the door, and Althea went to answer it.

Don't let him in! Felicia wanted to shout. But the words wouldn't come. She sat in paralyzed horror as Uncle Horace pushed into the room, his face haggard and clothes shredded. Felicia couldn't move a muscle or make the slightest sound, even though she knew what was coming.

Run, Auntie! She tried to scream a warning, but nothing happened. The otherworldly entity appeared, and she watched helpless as the whole terrible scene played out.

If only she could do something! There had to be a way to change things. *Please! Not this! Not again!*

Felicia woke, pulse racing, body clenched like a fist. She gasped, her heart breaking for the thousandth time, tears coursing down her cheeks.

But this awakening was different. Islen was there holding her, gently stroking her back, and murmuring words of comfort. Felicia leaned into the healing embrace, allowing Islen's warmth and kindness to ground her in the present moment. The dream gradually faded, and they both fell back asleep.

~*~

The next leg of the journey took them through the Dagger Glades, an area of rock formations so sharp they could cut through clothing or flesh, if a person wasn't careful to avoid contact. These were followed by a series of long lakes, with water as dark and transparent as black sapphires.

Some regions supported a bounty of colorful life, while others remained barren. Recent volcanic activity seemed to be a factor, as was proximity to water. The ever-changing landscape served to keep Felicia alert and interested over the many hours of travel time. She felt grateful for this and also for the frequent long walks she'd taken in the past—along the seashore and bird watching—as they helped her prepare for this trek.

It was near their destination of the Nemurithain clanhold, when the travelers encountered the Floating Death. They had just come through a narrow stone gorge that opened into a dark and desolate cavern. Felicia was about to activate a glow globe to better light their way, when Islen raised her hand in warning.

"Be still," she whispered, gazing ahead.

Around a bend in the cavern came floating a swarm of jellyfish-like creatures, pulsing vibrant green, with streaks of glowing amber-orange on their hoods and tentacles. They must have numbered in the hundreds, filling the space from cavern floor all the way to the ceiling. Some were as large as armchairs, while many smaller ones thronged around them.

Felicia watched their serene progress, utterly transfixed. How could anything so soft

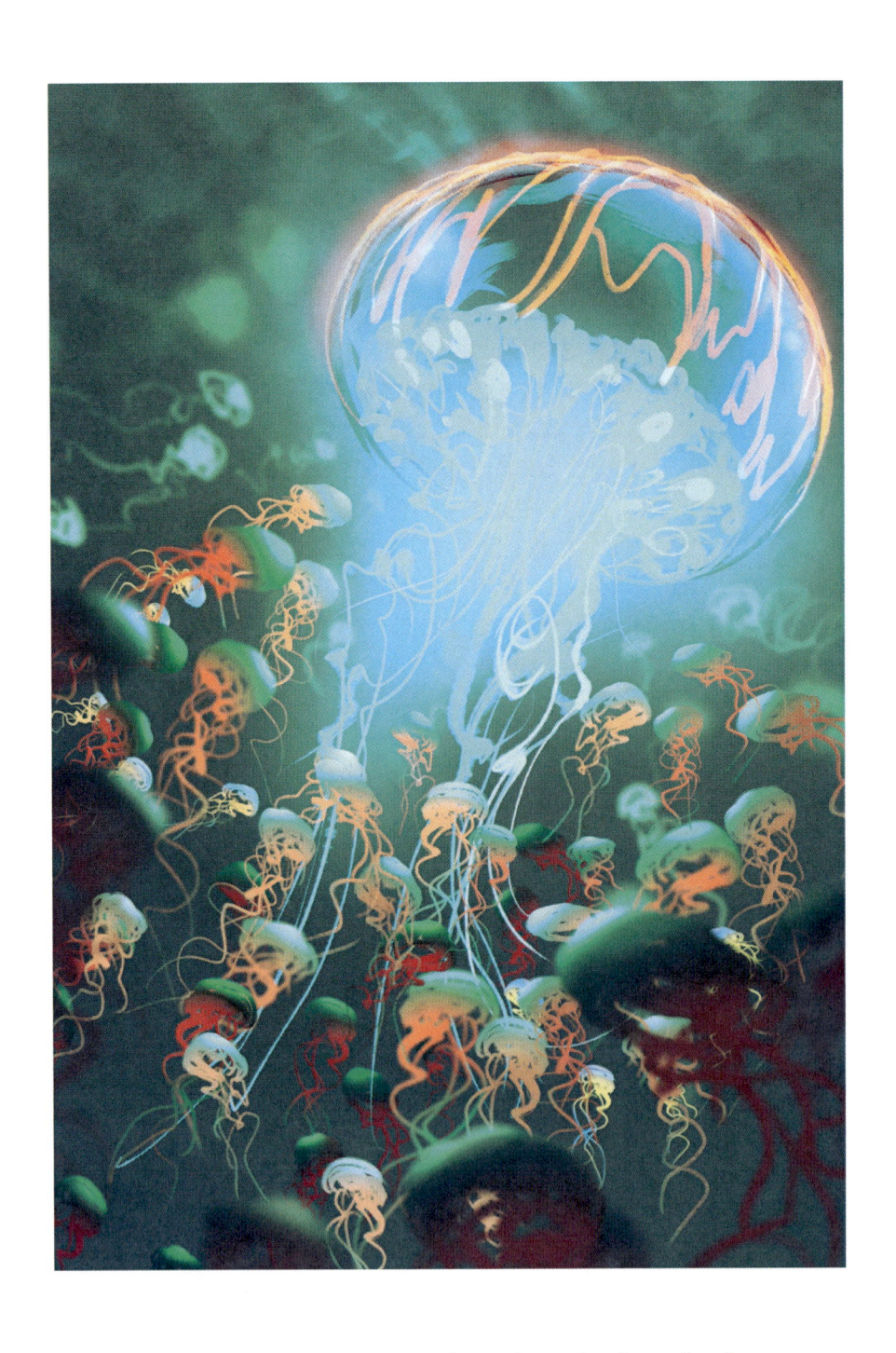

They must have numbered in the hundreds

and lovely pose such a threat? But they weren't called the Floating Death in jest. If she harbored any doubts about their deadliness, the next few moments made things clear.

A wooly tyroon, with six legs and three spiraling horns, came skittering down a side passage into the cavern. Close on its heels ran a dark-furred challirra, all teeth and claws. The predator looked ready to tackle its prey, but the Floating Death closed in first.

The tyroon bleated loudly as stinging tentacles enveloped it. The challirra leapt away, fleeing up the side passage just in time. A mass of the jellyfish-like creatures undulated around the struggling tyroon, until its movements ceased, and the cavern fell silent.

No one fancied suffering the same fate.

"Is there a different route to your clanhold?" Felicia whispered, barely moving her lips.

"No," GT answered. "Sometimes I've had to hide in the rocks for ages, waiting for the swarm to move on. I don't know any way to drive them off."

"My grandmother taught me a powerful repelling song," Islen offered. "It works on most pests and predators, though not with orvits, pernicious ukluffs, or gnats for some reason. It might be worth a try here."

"That sounds good," GT said. "I would hate to waste time hiding, when we're so close to my home. And the swarm might not move for days."

"What do you think?" Islen asked Felicia. "Is it worth the risk?"

"Well…we're right here by the cavern entrance. Maybe you could try your song and see how they react, while we still have a chance to escape back the way we came."

Islen nodded. "If it looks like my song is working, we should walk slowly through the cavern, drawing as little attention as possible. Quick movements might trigger their attack reflexes."

"Agreed."

Pulling her shoulders back and lifting her chin, Islen began to sing. There seemed to be words, though not in a language Felicia recognized. Neither was the melody like anything she'd heard before.

Islen's voice soared and vibrated, sounding sometimes high and haunting like a flute and other times throaty and rich as a cello. The effect was eerily poignant. The Floating Death responded, gradually drifting higher toward the cavern ceiling. This left a clear space of ten or twelve feet along the ground.

Felicia eased forward, following Islen as she began to walk—vividly aware of the swaying tentacles almost within arm's reach above their heads. Adrenaline coursed through her body, heart pounding and palms sweating.

Each time Islen paused in the song—to catch her breath or clear her throat—the Floating Death began to descend. And each time she quickly picked up the singing again, with even greater volume.

By the time they reached the next cavern—clear of any apparent danger—Felicia felt more than a little giddy. They had run the gauntlet and survived! Hurrah!

Although the experience had been frightening, it was also oddly exhilarating. The unearthly spectacle of the Floating Death—glowing like emerald lanterns in the dark—mingled with the aching beauty of Islen's song, had deeply affected her.

Now, Felicia gazed in wonder at her Nyarran friend. How marvelous she was! So brave. So wise and kind. So very, very appealing.

"Islen…would it be all right if I kiss you?" Felicia spoke the words before doubt could cause her to hesitate.

"Oh!" Islen's surprised expression dissolved into a wide grin. "Yes. I'd like that."

Felicia set GT carefully on a boulder, before turning her back on him and drawing Islen close. The two women's lips met, their breath mingling sweetly, as their hearts beat in perfect time with one another. Few things in life felt unquestionably right, but this was one of them.

CHAPTER SEVEN

Felicia hadn't expected the clanhold gatekeeper to be quite so BIG. The creature was easily the size of a whale, with a head like an angler fish and the body of a wingless dragon. A pattern of red and black speckled its armored hide, while teeth the size of butcher's knives glinted in its gaping maw.

The gatekeeper watched them approach, as yet making no move to intercept. It lashed a long forked tail, sending small rocks and cave dust flying into the air. A low growl reverberated from its massive throat, as its close-set eyes burned menacingly.

When Felicia stepped over some invisible line, the creature lunged forward, coming within a few feet of her face. She flung up her arm defensively, washed in the fetid heat of the monster's breath.

"Stand down, gatekeeper!" GT shouted from his perch on Felicia's shoulder. "It is I, The Great and Terrible Xtholubahn Nemurithain Brathoss. And these two are friends of the clan. Let us enter."

Red and black speckled its armored hide

The creature ceased growling and backed away, its head bowed. Felicia lowered her arm, hand trembling from the scare she'd received.

"That's quite a welcoming committee you've got there," she said. "I'd hate to see what happens to uninvited guests."

"We strongly discourage uninvited guests." GT grimaced. "Your uncle was one too many."

"Yes, of course. I'm sorry for making a poor joke."

"No apologies needed. And rest assured, you will always be a welcome visitor with my family."

"Thank you."

The Nemurithain clanhold sat in a cavern filled with stalagmites and stalactites. These formations glittered with rare mineral deposits and spikes of selenite crystal. The clan had carved their dwellings into the stalagmites, with little round windows shining like the twinkling lights of fairyland.

Felicia was thoroughly enchanted. That is, until hundreds of tiny Brathoss came rushing out of their homes to welcome GT home. They crowded around Islen's and Felicia's feet, cheering, as GT stood on her shoulder, holding the Crown of Visions aloft.

While the clan's joy was delightful, Felicia couldn't help a rising anxiety about so many little beings all jostling for space around her—some even climbing onto her boots for a better view. She didn't dare move an inch, for fear of crushing somebody.

"You're welcome to stay for our celebratory feast," GT said, speaking directly into her ear so as to be heard over the whooping crowd. "It will only take a few hours to prepare."

"Thank you, but I should travel on to Ellethon without delay. As it is, I'm not sure I'll get back to Port Lorence in time for work on Monday. And I don't want to lose my job."

What she didn't tell him was how uneasy it made her, standing like a giant among his people. If she stayed for hours, trying to avoid killing or injuring someone just might give her a heart attack.

"I understand." GT paused, searching for the right words. "My friendship is yours for life, Felicia Fisk. But now, I must remain here, to see my sister made chieftain. Though I had previously offered to go with you to Ellethon, I am sure Islen can serve in my stead."

"I will miss you," Felicia said. "No one is truer or more courageous of heart. It has been an honor traveling with you."

"May we meet again." He gave her cheek a fond pat before turning to speak his farewells with Islen.

And so they parted company, Felicia and Islen traveling on toward the Chrysolite Forest—location of the nearest Aldrahen waypost. For Ellethon was not a city to be reached by any common roads. Powerful spells cloaked the Adrahen capital in protective mists, closing the way to all but those with proper birthright or special permission.

A waypost would allow Felicia to communicate remotely with an Aldrahen official and make a request for entry. She doubted they would refuse, considering the treasure stored in her coat pocket. Surely they'd be thrilled to get the Prism Wand back.

The Chrysolite Forest still lay several miles farther on, when the two women finally stopped for a rest. As they ate a light meal, Felicia admired the view. Before them stretched a broad open area carpeted with blooming glimmerweirs. Although these plant-animal hybrids appeared like pale pink flowers, their seeds fluttered away on fragile petal wings—as if filling the air with rosy butterflies.

Through the gentle dance of their flight, a figure came riding. The steed was a great gray kiniyr, elk-like but larger, with shining silver eyes and tall antlers. The rider appeared to be a young Human woman. As she rode closer, Felicia noticed glowing symbols tattooed up her arm. She wore a simple tunic and leggings, her brown hair hanging in dozens of tight braids.

"I bet she's a changeling scout for the Aldrahen," Islen said. "She might be able to get us permission to enter Ellethon. It'd save us another half-day of walking to reach the waypost."

"That would be good." Felicia began packing away their food. "Let's go talk to her."

Denizens of the Dark explained how Aldrahen sometimes went to the surface world and took Human babies. They raised these changelings to be their servants, scouts, and

The rider appeared to be a young Human woman

other positions deemed unpleasant or troublesome. In recent times they'd begun limiting their selection to abandoned infants who might otherwise die. This by no means excused their exploitation of Humans, but it made the practice slightly less despicable.

The young woman riding the kiniyr was indeed a changeling. As Felicia made introductions and explained their situation, the scout didn't dismount or remove her hand from the long knife at her belt.

To prove her sincerity, Felicia withdrew the Prism Wand from her coat pocket and showed it to the changeling. The woman seemed duly impressed and quickly activated an engraved metal band around her wrist, using it to contact her supervisor. After several back and forth exchanges, Felicia and Islen were granted permission to enter Ellethon, with the scout ordered to escort them in.

She offered each woman a hand up, to climb on her great steed's back. Islen went first, sitting directly behind the changeling, with Felicia in the rear. She wrapped her arms around Islen's waist to keep from falling when the kiniyr trotted forward.

After riding less than an hour—the scout remaining stern and silent—they reached a dense wall of mist, crackling with magical energy. The effect was rather like bolts of lightning but dark rather than bright. The hair stood up on the back of Felicia's neck, and she wondered if it had been a mistake to come here.

The changeling called out a series of arcane words, raising her arm with the glowing tattoos. The symbols on her skin flashed brighter for an instant, and the mists parted, drawing back to reveal a narrow path leading off into the distance.

"I hope we don't regret this," Felicia whispered to Islen.

"No chance. I've always wanted to see Ellethon. And now I get to go there with you. What could be better?"

Felicia leaned forward and kissed Islen's cheek. "That's just what I needed to hear. Thank you."

~*~

Ellethon appeared out the mist, a glory of tall towers and delicate spires. The city looked to be made from polished obsidian, glossy, dark, and full of sharp edges. Light spilled from elaborately paneled windows, shaped into arches, diamonds, ovals, navettes, and pendeloques, faceted like the gem cuts they mimicked. And behind it all, the menacing backdrop of mist crackled and thrummed with magic.

Only a scattering of pedestrians could be seen along the streets. These were primarily Human changelings, each with a line of glowing tattoos running up their right arm. Most seemed busy with an appointed task, and none spared more than a glance at the newcomers riding past.

The few Aldrahen stood out from their servants like storks among pigeons. Not only

A glory of tall towers and delicate spires

were they taller, but their skin and their long straight hair all shimmered silver, as if lit from within. In fact, everything about the Aldrahen was silver, except their exquisite jewel-toned garments and their indigo eyes.

Felicia and Islen were taken to a lodging house where they could rest and refresh while waiting for an audience with the High Lord. Apparently it was to him the Prism Wand rightfully belonged.

Their suite was luxurious, designed with a refined sensibility and attention to detail. The headboards of the two beds were intricate silverwork, shaped into spider webs, sparkling with tiny diamonds of dew. The coverlets were ice blue satin, with royal blue cushions and pillowcases. This same color scheme carried throughout the space, with hints of cream and gold to break up any monotony for the eye.

Felicia wandered through the suite, admiring the various decorative elements, from the nature-themed tapestries, to the chandeliers like crystal rain. She was particularly drawn to the statuettes of a wulvirri pack, carved from bluish-white stone, arranged along the fireplace mantle. She touched the figurines, following the graceful wolf-like forms captured by the artist.

"I used to dream of seeing wulvirri," she told Islen. "*The Denizens of the Dark* has a gorgeous illustration of them, looking so wild and magnificent. I know the Aldrahen trap them to keep as pets, but it seems a terrible shame, to put a chain around the neck of such an animal...even if the chain is made of silver and gold."

"I think that practice fell out of favor," Islen responded, laying back on one of the palatial beds. "This new High Lord came into power a few years ago, and I hear he's a reformer. Gossip says he may even stop the taking of Human changelings."

"I hope he does!" Felicia came and stretched out next to Islen, sinking into the feather-soft mattress. "I'll feel better returning the Prism Wand, if I know he's not a heartless tyrant."

"Apparently he's quite ethical...for an Aldrahen Lord." Islen gave a dry chuckle. "Which, granted, isn't the strongest commendation. The Aldrahen haven't been very good neighbors to anyone in the Dark Realm. But at least this new monarch is trying to improve things."

"I'm nervous about meeting him," Felicia admitted. "I don't know any of the protocols, and I'd hate to accidentally offend someone in this place. They seem so powerful."

"I wouldn't worry too much." Islen propped up on an elbow and reached out to stroke Felicia's hair. "You're returning a precious royal heirloom. How could they not be pleased with you? You're the hero of the day." Her long fingers caressed Felicia's cheek. "And after we're done in Ellethon, maybe we can track down some wild wulvirri for you to see. A few packs live near the Graytooth Mountains, west of here. How does that sound?"

Felicia smiled. "Wonderful." Right now she couldn't think about work schedules or other practical concerns. Not with Islen so close, gazing at her with those entrancing amber eyes. "And how does the possibility of kissing sound to you?"

"I am definitely in favor of it."

For a while the women were pleasantly occupied with each other, the rest of the world fading from their awareness. It had been a long time since Felicia experienced such easy intimacy, if indeed she ever had. Eventually they drifted off to sleep, curled together in blissful comfort.

CHAPTER EIGHT

The first to wake, Felicia lay peacefully, savoring the sensation of holding Islen in her arms. All was quiet, her mind and body relaxed. Her heart swelled with happiness, as she contemplated the unexpected blessings received these past few days.

Gradually, a faint but insistent tickling in the back of her throat began to distract Felicia. A familiar coppery tang, alerted her to the presence of magic. It was very subtle—so much so she'd failed to notice it until now.

Curious, she rose from the bed, careful not to disturb Islen's sleep. She walked slowly around the suite, following her sixth sense. Of course Ellethon would be bursting with magic, but this felt close and definitely active.

At last she pinpointed the source, a cluster of droplet shaped diamonds, at the center of each bed's headboard. Around these pulsed tiny ripples of sorcery, almost too soft to detect.

Felicia closed her eyes, turning the spell in her mind. The purpose was elusive at first, so finely woven was it. She could barely discern the pattern, but after several minutes, she understood. This was a surveillance spell, meant to listen in on—and possibly observe—whatever occurred in the room.

How rude!

Irritation flared. The Aldrahen had no business violating her privacy. She'd come here in good faith and expected better from her hosts.

Felicia reexamined the spell, locating a weak point in the outermost layer of symbols. She reached with her will and tweaked it, ever so gently—not enough to destroy the whole thing, just enough to deactivate it.

The process came easier than with her uncle's wardings. Perhaps because she was getting back in practice—like riding a bicycle again after many years. It certainly felt good, that same invigorating tingling filling her as the last time.

Buoyed by her success, Felicia dressed and tidied up as best she could. Unfortunately there was no bathtub or sink. The only water to be found was in a large ewer, set on a tray with crystal goblets. Near these rested a bowl of little silver balls.

At first she thought they might be fancy soaps, but they proved impervious to water. More than anything else, they resembled transportable glow globes, except for their opaque metallic finish.

She spoke the activation for glow globes. "Luminn." Nothing happened. Perhaps they were simply ornamental.

Without other options, Felicia settled on splashing her face with water then brushing her hair and teeth. Thank goodness she'd had the sense to put a hairbrush and toothbrush in her coat pocket before leaving home. Too bad she hadn't added a change of clothes.

By then Islen woke up, and a sumptuous meal was delivered to their suite. As the two women ate together, they talked of this and that, eventually sharing what their lives had been like during the long years apart. Despite the decades of separation, the old bond felt strong between them, woven now with lovely new layers and threads of deeper connection.

It came as a bit a shock, when an imperious knocking sounded at the door. They'd both lost track of time, caught up as they were in each other's stories.

Felicia opened the door to a willowy Aldrahen woman, dressed in teal silk robes, embroidered with peacock feathers. Her silver hair was swept high, held by emerald and sapphire pins.

"The High Lord will see you now," she announced, looking down her fine nose at Felicia. "There is still time to cleanse yourself, before entering his presence." Her upper lip curled ever so slightly.

"I have cleaned up as much as your facilities allow," Felicia told her. "A proper wash would have been nice, but there's no bathtub. Perhaps they aren't the fashion in Ellethon?"

The Aldrahen's eyebrows rose. "Were cleansing orbs not provided with your suite?"

"Cleansing orbs? Do you mean those the little silver—"

The woman swept past her to retrieve the bowl of baubles. She lifted one over Felicia's head, popping it open between her thumb and forefinger, while speaking an arcane phrase.

Silver light washed down over Felicia, sparkling like water droplets in sunshine. Instantly her hair, skin, and clothes were clean and fresh. She felt utterly renewed and smelled sweet as apple blossoms.

"Oh! Thank you. I had no idea..." She turned grinning to Islen. "You've got to try one of these. They're splendid."

"Your Nyarran friend will not require a cleansing, as she cannot accompany you to the audience chamber," the Aldrahen woman said.

"Why not?"

"For security reasons, we only allow one foreigner at a time to meet with the High Lord. Since you are the one bearing the Prism Wand, that person will be you. It is a rare privilege for any Human."

Felicia frowned, ready to argue. But Islen stepped close, giving her hand a reassuring squeeze.

"It's not a problem," she said. "I don't want to meet Mr. Fancy Pants anyway. I'll be fine waiting here."

"Are you sure?"

"Yes. It gives me a chance to finish that excellent cavefish in mushroom sauce...not to mention the sweet truffles."

"Very well." Felicia picked up her coat, from where it lay over the back of a chair, and began to put it on.

"You cannot wear that to the audience chamber," the Aldrahen woman told her, speaking as if to a dimwitted child. "It is enchanted, with at least three different spells, possibly more."

"I'm not here to assassinate your High Lord," Felicia snapped, nettled by the woman's disdain. "I'm trying to be *helpful*."

"Regardless. You will not wear that coat or bring anything with you except the Prism Wand. Have I spoken clearly enough for you to understand?"

Felicia gritted her teeth. "Yes. I understand."

"Good. Then we shouldn't keep the High Lord waiting."

~*~

The audience chamber looked nothing like Felicia expected. Based on the lodging house décor, she'd imagined something opulent, packed with rich furnishings and dazzling ornamentation. Instead the immense room was surprisingly stark.

The dark polished floor stretched from one end to the other, devoid of furniture. Tall windows lined both sides, providing a stunning view over the city. But they remained bare of draperies, sashes, or any other adornment. Only a massive tapestry, covering the far wall, leant any color to the space.

The image was arresting, at least fifty feet high, and nearly that much across. It featured an abstract pattern, combining elements of moth wings, butterfly wings, insect eyes, and antennae. Brilliant reds and golds contrasted with sage green, brown, and black, with here and there a burst of white. It was both symmetrical and organic, vibrant yet also imposing. Felicia had never seen anything like it.

At the base of this artistic marvel sat a bare dais, perfectly suited for a throne but lacking even a simple bench. There stood a tall Aldrahen man, dressed in long robes of cream brocade satin. His garments were embellished with hundreds—possibly thousands—of lustrous pearls, so that he seemed to glimmer like a star. He stood perfectly still, face unreadable, as Felicia and her haughty escort approached. Besides the three of them, the room was empty.

"My Lord, this is the Human who brings you the Prism Wand," the Aldrahen woman announced, sinking into a graceful curtsy.

Felicia copied the movement, without making an utter fool of herself. Silk robes definitely suited the performance better. Her turtleneck and trousers felt ridiculously casual, but at least they were now clean.

"Thank you, Lady Orietha," the High Lord responded, with a slight nod of his head. "If you would be so kind as to check on the item we spoke of earlier. And if it is ready, bring it to us here."

The image was arresting, over fifty feet high

"Of course, My Lord." Lady Orietha curtsied again and departed.

"I noticed you studying the dais a moment ago." The High Lord now addressed his words to Felicia. "Were you expecting a throne, perhaps?"

"Yes, actually. It looks like the perfect spot for one. And I've noticed that Aldrahen do enjoy their fine…uh…well, their…" She sputtered to a stop, suddenly aware of risking offense to her host.

"We are fond of our finery, to be sure," he said, with a light laugh. "And this room did hold a mighty throne, fit for a god to lounge upon. It also housed a surplus of other furnishings, meant to divide up all who entered into their 'proper' strata. The highest born at the front, with the best of everything, descending in richness and quality to the very back, where the lowest of nobles lurked." He fixed her with his sharp gaze, waiting for a response.

"Am I right in supposing you had it all removed when you took power?" she asked.

"Indeed," his pale lips pulled into a smile. "I wanted a fresh start…clarity, simplicity, equality, and other admirable ideals. Sadly, the rest of my people were not so inclined. Clearing out this audience chamber was the easiest change I've made. The rest has been like herding a hundred wild challirras through a single narrow door."

"It is good that you keep trying, My Lord. The betterment of your society is a worthy goal."

"How ironic, to receive encouragement from a Human. But then again, you are that rarest of things, a Human with genuine principals, as evidenced by your return of the Prism Wand."

Felicia struggled with an urge to argue the relative merit of Human principals when compared to those of Aldrahen. In the end, she decided discretion was the better part of valor. He had diplomatically reminded her of the wand, and now she should return the heirloom and be done. It was time to be heading home, if she wanted to keep her job.

"Here it is, My Lord." She handed him the precious crystal rod. "I am truly sorry that my uncle took it."

"Yes...a most unfortunate episode in my father's reign. But now the Wand has come home again. I am most grateful to you." He inclined his head in acknowledgement of her service. "And here is Lady Orietha, with her usual perfect timing."

The Aldrahen woman approached, carrying an elegantly simple staff. The wood was of pale silvery hue, rubbed smooth as satin. The top bore a polished slate-blue stone, held in place with soft gray leather, which continued down, wrapping the wood for several inches and providing a comfortable handhold.

"This is our gift of thanks," the High Lord said, taking the staff and handing it to Felicia. "It is charmed so that the bearer will never stumble or fall, no matter how treacherous the terrain."

"Thank you! I didn't anticipate any reward. I just wanted to put things right. This is so generous, and such a useful item. I...I don't know what to say. Thank you."

The High Lord smiled graciously. "You are welcome. Now, is there anything else we can provide, before you depart?"

Felicia recognized a polite dismissal when she heard it, but one burning curiosity remained. She swallowed her caution and looked the High Lord in the eye.

"Might I ask what the Prism Wand is used for? I feel the power in it, but I can't for the life of me discern the purpose."

"Ah...so you are adept at sensing magic."

"She's also capable of dismantling," Lady Orietha informed him. "She broke the observation spell in her suite."

"I didn't break it," Felicia protested, heat rising to her cheeks. "I only deactivated it...though perhaps I should have done more. It's exceedingly rude to spy on your guests."

"My apologies." The High Lord seemed more embarrassed than remorseful. "We are forced to take precautions, in these unsettled times. But let me make amends. I will not only tell you what the Prism Wand does, I will show you."

"Is that wise, My Lord?" Lady Orietha objected. "She is a Human, after all."

"A Human who returned one of our greatest treasures, without expectation of reward. I see no harm in it, and I've waited a long time to try the Wand for myself."

Lady Orietha pressed her lips together, clearly unhappy but refraining from further comment.

The High Lord led Felicia from the audience chamber, down a hallway, and out to a courtyard. The far wall was elaborately carved, with symbols, swirls, and circles within circles. A high triple arch stood centered on the wall, though it framed nothing. The stone within the arch looked as solid and black as the rest of the palace exterior.

The High Lord flashed a surprisingly youthful grin and placed the wand into a slot on the wall. He uttered a string of arcane syllables, and the arch blazed with light. Symbols lit with white fire, as the center opened into a brilliant vortex.

Cold shivered over Felicia's skin. Freezing mist drifted across the courtyard, sparkling with tiny particles of ice. This was clearly some kind of portal, but where to?

"The Prism Wand is the key to our most prized gateway," the High Lord explained. "It transports a person anywhere they can picture in detail. As long as the place is well-known to them, so the magic can read their thoughts and complete the journey accurately, the destinations are limitless."

"Astonishing!" Felicia marveled at the power required for such a portal.

"If you like, this can be your way home," he offered. "Just a few steps and you'll return to the surface world, at any place of your choosing."

Symbols lit with white fire, as the center opened

"That would be tremendously helpful. I've been worried about making it back in time."

"Then worry no more. You may depart now, if that suits you."

"Oh...well...you see, my companion is waiting for me, back in the guest suite, and I have some other matters to attend to, before leaving the Dark Realm. Would it be acceptable for me to return later, and use the portal then?"

"Of course. Whenever you are ready."

"Thank you. I expect it won't be more than two or three days. I do so appreciate your kindness."

Felicia's mind spun with possibilities. With an instant return to the surface world available, she and Islen could spend more time together, exploring the Dark Realm. It wasn't every day a person had this kind of opportunity. She didn't plan on wasting it.

CHAPTER NINE

Lady Orietha escorted Felicia and Islen through Ellethon toward the west gate. From there, they could hike to the places most favorable for wulvirri sightings.

The Aldrahen city lay in an immense open region at the heart of the Dark Realm. This area stretched more than a hundred miles across, including the Chrysolite Forest, the Graytooth Mountains, and more. Here, the warren of connecting caverns gave way to a vast dim expanse. The feeling of being underground almost entirely vanished, as the space was so large, no ceiling was visible in the shadowy twilight that hung over everything.

"I will go no farther," Lady Orietha told them. Beyond lay the outskirts of Ellethon, an area separated from the rest of the city by a low curving wall. The barrier was purely symbolic, as most anyone could climb over. But it marked the end of the 'respectable' neighborhoods and the beginning of the slums.

"Simply follow that road," she said, gesturing to a narrow lane which wound through clusters of sagging tenements. "It will take you through the changeling quarter to the west gate. Show this to the guard on duty. He will open the mists for you."

Lady Orietha handed Felicia a flat metal disk, slightly smaller than her palm. A hole was cut from the center, and around this four symbols glowed.

"When you wish to return to Ellethon, press that key to any waypost, and the mists will part." Lady Orietha gave them both a steely look. "Take good care of it. We rarely lend keys to outsiders and will expect it returned in a timely manner."

"Of course," Felicia assured. "The key will be safe with us."

"See that it is." Lady Orietha turned her back on them and strode swiftly toward the palace.

Felicia watched her leave with relief. "That woman makes me feel like an uncouth little toad...one she'd happily squash."

"That's the Aldrahen for you," Islen sympathized, "vain and superior to a fault."

As they set off through the changeling quarter, Felicia was struck by how different it appeared from the rest of Ellethon. No lofty spires and gleaming stonework here. Instead the wooden tenements looked slapped together, one story sitting haphazardly atop another. Even the ground was marshy, releasing an odor of decay, which added to the general squalor.

A sluggish channel of water wound through the buildings, reflecting the flickering

The wooden tenements looked slapped together

lights in dull orange. A lone changeling poled his boat over the murky stream, his face a picture of grim endurance.

The place seemed oddly silent, with hardly anyone out and about. A few faces appeared at windows, furtively watching Felicia and Islen pass by, but the doors remained firmly closed.

No one approached the two travelers, until a short distance from the west gate a young changeling boy ran up to Felicia and pressed a piece of parchment into her hand. Before she could speak to him, he ran off into the dark alleyways.

"What does it say?" Islen asked.

Felicia read and reread the words, baffled. "Someone wants to meet me at the Oracle Tree." She checked her watch. "In about twenty hours from now. They claim to know the 'truth' about my parents' deaths. They also say I must arrive alone, that any companions must stop and wait for me before the final ravine. If not, this individual won't speak with me at all."

"Any idea who could have written it?"

"None." Felicia glanced around curiously. "How would a changeling know anything about my family?"

"Maybe your uncle had a contact in Ellethon."

"Perhaps." Felicia considered. "There's only one sure way to find out."

"It could be a trap of some kind," Islen warned.

"But what could they hope to gain?"

Islen glanced meaningfully at the side of Felicia's coat that hid the magic pocket. She did carry valuable artifacts. But who in Ellethon knew about them?

"Let's not discuss it anymore here," Felicia said. "We can't be sure who might be listening."

Islen nodded her agreement, and so they continued on to the west gate in silence.

~*~

Once the two women were well beyond the mists of Ellethon, Felicia raised the subject again.

"It's impossible to know if the person who wrote that note has good intentions. But I have to admit, I'm curious what they have to say. I'd already been toying with the idea of visiting the Oracle Tree, since we're in this part of the Dark Realm. It seems a shame to pass up the chance for a magical vision."

"The Graytooth Mountains are high and craggy," Islen told her. "They'll test your stamina and courage both."

"Well, I'm reasonably fit...even more so after these past few days. I know I'm not as agile as you, but I do have this charmed staff the Aldrahen gave me. There's also the rope and grappling hooks I took from my uncle's hoard."

"You're really determined to do this?"

"Strangely, yes." Felicia found herself grinning. "I guess I'm developing a taste for adventure after all."

Islen returned her smile. "It appears I've been a bad influence on you."

"Oh, definitely. The very worst kind of influence."

They shared a quick laugh and a kiss, before Felicia sobered. "I think it would be wise if I hid the treasures and the Aldrahen key somewhere safe, before I meet this mystery person at the Oracle Tree. If it is a trap, I don't want any of those items falling into the wrong hands."

"Good idea," Islen affirmed. "You're even starting to think like an adventurer."

The two women continued on their way, soon reaching the foothills of the Graytooth Mountains. As they climbed through increasingly challenging terrain, Felicia kept her eyes open for an appropriate location to stash her valuables. After a few hours she spotted a gorge, notable for a distinct tumble of rocks near the opening. This was a place she could surely find again.

"Over there," she told Islen. "That's where I want to hide the artifacts and key."

They left the trail marked for pilgrims to the Oracle Tree and clambered over boulders into the gorge. Here the shadows gathered thick, with little bioluminescent life of any kind. As they progressed, Felicia caught glimpses of creatures moving up ahead—something bright and wolf-like.

"Wulvirri," she whispered, clasping Islen's hand.

The pack was small in number, only four adults that she could see, though they might have pups back at the den. The animals looked healthy, with long silky fur and tails like snowy plumes. They shone blue-white in the darkness, lifting their delicate muzzles to scent the air, their silver eyes keen. Felicia watched spellbound until the wulvirri loped away, disappearing further up the gorge.

"That was breathtaking," she murmured, "an absolute dream come true."

"Wulvirri are believed to be good luck," Islen told her.

"Then this was an omen. We've found the right spot for our stash, and everything will turn out well."

After hiding the valuables, the two women retraced their steps to the trail and continued on toward the Oracle Tree. Soon they were glad for the grappling hooks and rope, as rocky cliffs and steep-sided ravines blocked their way. Felicia's arms and legs ached, her hands developing blisters. And still, there were miles to go.

When at last they stopped to rest, the two women took turns sleeping and keeping watch. The mountains remained quiet and desolate, with no sign of other travelers. Felicia struggled to stay awake during her turn at watch, her eyelids drooping and head sagging.

Once, far off in the gloom above her, she thought she heard a great beast fly over. She peered up, unable to see through the constant dusk. Had she merely imagined the sound of mighty wings beating?

The route to the Oracle Tree grew more punishing as they continued, and Felicia began to wonder if her stamina would hold long enough to reach their destination. Still, she wasn't ready to give up, not after having come this far. Life as a librarian might not have prepared her for such a journey, but she had a cord of steel running through her center. The Graytooth Mountains were not going to get the better of Felicia Fisk!

She repeated this affirmation, as she hauled herself up yet another cliff, hands burning with pain, body aching like she'd been pounded with a meat tenderizing mallet. When she finally reached the top and saw they had arrived, her relief felt incandescent.

They stood on a dim plateau, split by a deep ravine. Thankfully a bridge spanned the gap, as any other crossing looked near impossible. This must be the 'final ravine' referred to in Felicia's mysterious note. Islen would need to wait on the near side, and watch the meeting from a distance.

On the far side, at the crest of small rocky slope, the Oracle Tree stood. It had grown large over the millennia, with a trunk as wide as a bus and thick gnarled branches. Magic crackled around its leafless crown, lit with swirls of purple, green, and blue energy.

"Are you ready for this?" Islen asked.

"As ready as I'll ever be, though I don't see anyone here to meet me."

"They could be standing around the other side of the tree waiting. It's wide enough to hide several people."

"Not a comforting thought."

"I can come with you," Islen offered.

"No. I've got my coat and umbrella. And you can see if I'm in trouble. At the speed you run, it'll only take a minute to reach me. Everything will be fine."

For now, Felicia kept the umbrella in her magic coat pocket, as she needed one hand free to hold a glow globe and the other for her charmed staff. The footing on the bridge looked uneven, with no barrier between its narrow width and the seemingly endless depths of the ravine.

She pulled her coat's hood up for extra protection, activated the glow globe, and started across.

She needed one hand free to hold a glow globe

CHAPTER TEN

When Felicia reached the Oracle Tree, and a figure stepped out from behind the trunk, she could barely contain her surprise. This person's face was covered with the same custom gas mask as the man in the library. But even more alarming, he wore an all too familiar yellow coat and held a yellow umbrella exactly like her red one.

"Uncle Horace?" she gasped. But no, it couldn't be. She'd identified her uncle's corpse in the morgue. He was well and truly dead.

"Close, but no cigar," the mystery man said, giving a dry laugh. "The name is Cedric Ramsford, and I'm your cousin."

"I don't have any cousins."

"Oh, but you do. Horace may not have acknowledged me publically, but I am most certainly his son."

Felicia absorbed this news, wondering if Cedric was the one who sent thugs to spy on her house and ambush her that night by the river. She dropped her staff and glow globe, retrieving the umbrella from her coat pocket and holding it with both hands. The last time she used the stun function, the recoil caught her unawares. This time she'd be ready.

"Don't look so distressed," Cedric soothed. "I'm not here to cause any trouble."

"What do you want?"

"Just to set the family record straight and connect with my only living relative. You'd like that wouldn't you, sweet cousin? Blood is thicker than water, after all."

"Stop patronizing me, and get to the point." She didn't trust this fellow one bit.

"There's no cause to be rude." He shook his head. "I expected better manners from the only legitimate Fisk offspring. Didn't your parents raise you better than that?"

"Your note said you knew the truth about their deaths. I'd like to hear it."

"Very well. Horace magically rigged their car brakes to go out at a specific spot along their planned route. That way he got rid of them both cleanly, so he could inherit the estate. The whole thing was masterfully executed, and no one ever found the evidence to charge him with murder."

Despite his grating manner, Cedric's words rang true. In her heart of hearts Felicia had long suspected foul play. This simply confirmed her instincts.

"How did you learn about this?" she asked.

"Horace told me, during one of our rare 'friendly' visits. He wasn't the easiest man to have for a father, as you can imagine. But there was a time when he seemed interested in passing on his legacy to me."

"What went wrong?" She couldn't help a certain macabre curiosity.

"We had a rather severe falling out, and things got heated…quite literally." He let out a barking laugh. "The old man tried to melt my face off with magic. That's why I wear this mask. I don't have his skill with illusions, and the burn scars are not pretty."

"I'm sorry. That must have been painful."

"It was. But I got my own back on him, in a very final sort of way."

"You're the one who killed him?" A shiver ran over Felicia's scalp. She shouldn't underestimate what Cedric was capable of.

"Oh yes. I finished him off. It seemed only fitting."

"And now you've come here, all this way through the Dark Realm, just to reveal the truth about my parents' deaths and to forge a familial bond with me?"

He cocked his head to the side. "You don't believe that for a second, do you?"

"No. I don't." Felicia tightened her grip on the umbrella handle.

"Well you see, the old man wasn't much for sharing his treasures. He did like to brag though, and he told me all about the artifacts he'd stashed somewhere around the estate. I tried finding them, but had no luck, until I hit on the idea of trailing you. The plan seemed to work like a charm, and I thought it would be as easy as taking candy from a baby...or books from a librarian, as the case may be."

He chuckled at his own joke before continuing. "Turns out I underestimated your resourcefulness. When you bested those three men I sent after you, I came to an important realization. If you want something done right, you've got to do it yourself."

Cedric clearly loved the sound of his own voice, but Felicia was quickly growing tired of it.

"You're wasting your time," she told him. "I don't have anything on me. The only item of value has already been given back to its owner."

"Ah, my sweet cousin. You don't lie very well. Not enough practice, I'd wager."

"If you have connections in Ellethon, then you'll know I've returned the Prism Wand to the Aldrahen." She took a gamble that Cedric might be unaware of GT and the Crown of Visions. He certainly wouldn't learn about them from her.

"Sadly I didn't catch up with you in time to prevent that little setback," he said. "But the Prism Wand isn't much use, practically speaking, without access to the portal in Ellethon. It's more a vanity object really, a chance to humiliate those insufferable Aldrahen. There are several other artifacts that interest me more."

"I'm not going to give you anything, Cedric. Horace caused a lot of misery in his lifetime, but that legacy ended with his death. You need to find a different path."

"I was afraid you'd be stubborn. So I brought along a little insurance...to hedge my bets, in a manner of speaking." He pointed to a strap of scaled leather around his neck. "This doesn't look like much, but I assure you, it's Horace's most valuable treasure...an honest to goodness Dragon Collar. In fact, this is the very item we fought over, the day he died."

Felicia couldn't detect any magic about the leather band, until Cedric spoke the activating words. Then a wave of power exploded outward, rippling like intense heat through the air. Within moments a mighty beating of wings could be heard, and a crimson dragon appeared, flying up from beyond the cliff. The creature's wingspan must have stretched thirty feet, its scales glinting like rubies. Smoke and flame billowed from its mouth.

Cedric laughed gleefully, unafraid for his safety. He merely raised his yellow umbrella, to deflect the shower of sparks—reveling in the command of such raw power.

The scene so stunned Felicia that she stood paralyzed with shock. Meanwhile the dragon swooped, tearing at the ravine's bridge with its massive talons. Islen, who had just begun to run across, darted back out of the way.

"You may not realize," Cedric shouted, "but most of Horace's best treasures are fireproof. I can collect them from your charred corpse later, once the pyrotechnics are over."

His words brought Felicia back to her senses. She pointed her umbrella toward Cedric and spoke the stun command. Energy pulsed out, knocking him back a few paces.

Cedric laughed gleefully, unafraid for his safety

Unfortunately his warded coat provided ample protection.

Next she tried targeting the dragon, who had managed to destroy the center section of the bridge. The umbrella's power seemed to have no effect on the beast. It banked in a tight circle and flew low over Felicia, breathing a tempest of flame. She was engulfed in fire, the center of a blazing inferno, but the coat and umbrella shielded her.

Twice more the dragon attacked her, and the red coat disintegrated in a mess of stinking, smoldering wool. Few spells were strong enough to withstand repeated blasts of dragon fire. Even the umbrella was starting to burn, holes widening along the edges.

Cedric shouted a command to his monstrous servant. The dragon changed direction, focusing its fury on Islen, who picked her way through the rubble of the bridge, trying to cross the ravine. She ducked behind a boulder, escaping the worst of the flames, but her luck wouldn't hold forever.

Seeing Islen in imminent peril, something finally snapped inside Felicia. She refused to stand by helpless and watch another person dear to her be destroyed. Enough was enough! This had to stop now!

Rage boiled up within her, for all the injustices, all the havoc wreaked by these selfish bastards, both father and son. She let loose, no longer reining in the storm of her emotions. They surged through her, waking the buried depths of her power. Her limbs vibrated with it. Her eyes blazed. She saw everything in dagger-sharp clarity and knew exactly what needed to be done.

As the dragon circled, coming around for another barrage, Felicia focused on the cords of sorcery binding the beast's will to Cedric's commands. With her heightened awareness she could sense the dragon's anger, its struggle against the invisible chains of magic. The creature yearned for freedom, despising Cedric for enslaving it.

Felicia reached out at the apex of her power, cutting like a molten scythe through the binding spell. In one fell swoop it dropped away, the Dragon Collar crumbling to ash at Cedric's throat. He screamed as the winged beast, now freed from its thrall, plucked him up and carried him aloft, giving a thundering triumphant roar.

Her vision tunneling, Felicia staggered back against the trunk of the Oracle Tree. She'd never in all her life expended so much magical energy. Breaking a binding of that magnitude had taken everything in her. Now she sank to her knees, utterly depleted. The world went dark, as her head sagged against the rough tree bark.

Time lost all meaning. Silence surrounded Felicia as she floated in a starry indigo night. She seemed to be drifting through the cosmos, as if carried along by a vast invisible current, gentle yet inexorable.

At last it deposited her upon an unfamiliar shore. Radiance filled the sky, an ecstasy of

She saw everything in dagger-sharp clarity

color beyond any earthly dawn. The turf was soft and sweet-smelling beneath her feet, the air fresh and clear.

And then Felicia saw Althea, dressed in simple white, her fair hair pulled back in a long braid. Her aunt stood regal as a queen, back straight and chin high. Yet her face was filled with the warmth of kindness and the glow of true contentment.

"My beloved Felicia," she said opening her arms in welcome. "I am so glad to see you."

Felicia ran forward to hug Althea, astonishment and joy whirling within her.

"How am I here with you?" she asked. "What is this place?"

Althea smiled. "We are somewhere between, brought together by the Oracle Tree, so we might finally have a chance to say goodbye."

"This is a vision? But it feels so real."

"It is real." Althea leaned forward and kissed Felicia's brow. "You are so precious to me. I wish I could have been there, all these years, to share your delights and your despairs, but we don't often get to choose our time of passing."

"I've missed you so much. And I'm so sorry I couldn't save you. I would have given anything to change what happened."

"There was nothing you could have done," Althea assured. "The time has come to let it go, once and for all. I am at peace. And when, many years from now, your own passing comes, I'll be there to greet you, to guide you through the veil

Her aunt stood regal as a queen

to the other side." She put her arms around Felicia, holding her close. "All is well."

"I love you, Auntie."

"I love you, dear one."

At last they stepped apart.

"This is only goodbye for now," Althea reminded. "We will meet again."

"I'm so grateful. Thank you…for everything." Felicia's heart felt full enough to burst.

"Farewell, Felicia."

"Farewell, Auntie."

The vision faded, as she floated once more in velvety darkness. She felt herself surfacing, rising toward the solid weight of arms and legs and aching head. But right at the last, before regaining consciousness, Felicia received a brief glimpse of the future.

For an instant, she saw herself and Islen, standing on a high ridge. They both wore mountaineering gear, Felicia with her trusty Aldrahen staff, and Islen with ropes looped through the straps of her pack. Islen's arm rested affectionately around Felicia's shoulders, as together they gazed over a broad valley, toward a distant simmering volcano. They looked strong, exhilarated, and wonderfully alive.

"Felicia! Wake up." Islen's voice slipped into her awareness. "Everything is going to be all right. I'm here with you. The dragon left, after it ate that man in the yellow coat. We're safe. Please wake up."

Arms circled her, gently rocking. She awoke to Islen's face, golden eyes glossy with emotion, a relieved smile bringing out that lovely dimple at the corner of her mouth.

The healing and the promise of Felicia's two visions swept through her. It was as if she'd been set free and welcomed home, all in one breath—a closure to one life chapter and the wondrous beginning of another. The past was truly behind her, and the future beckoned, bright as a summer sunrise.

And so they live whole-heartedly ever after, enjoying many more grand adventures.

THE END

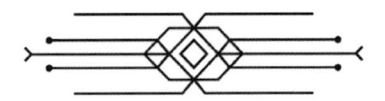

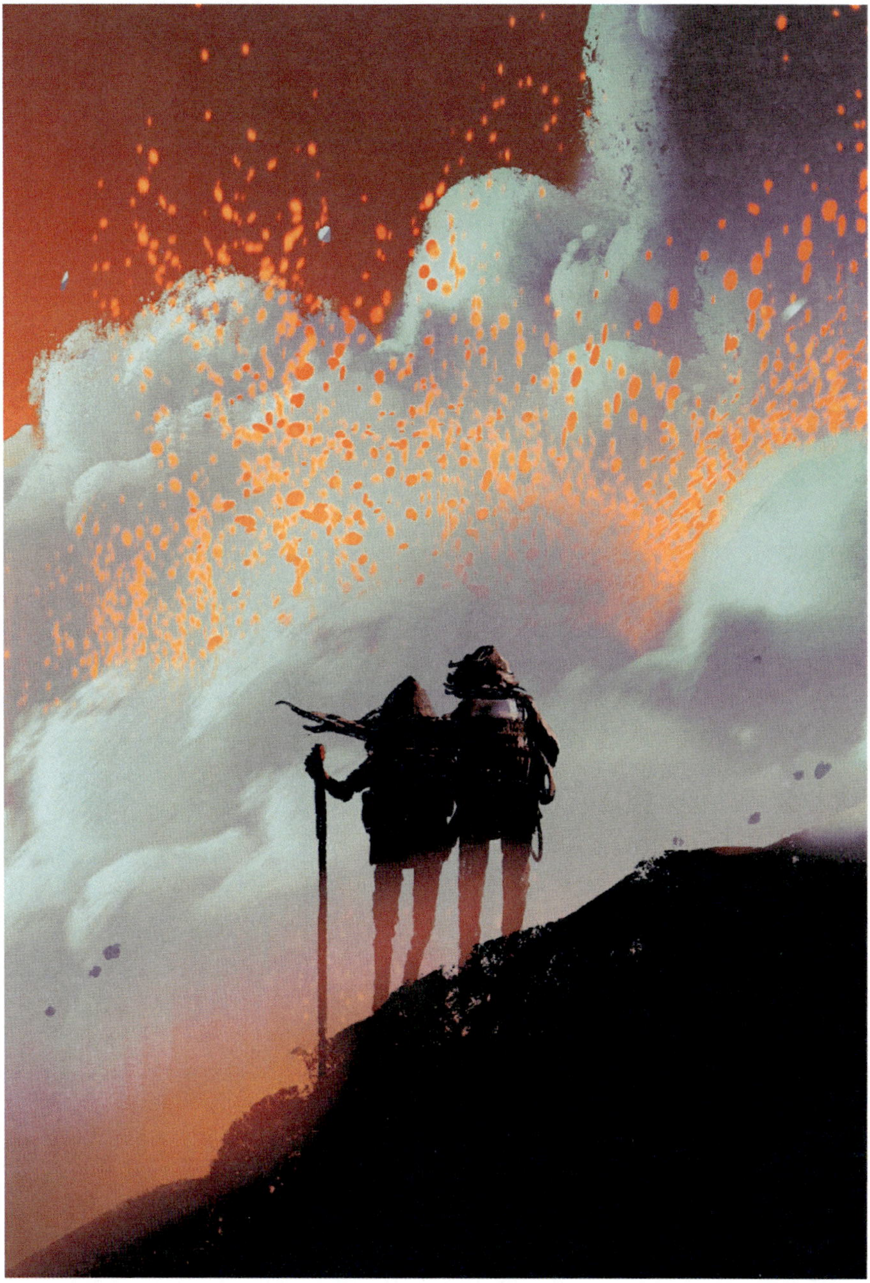

DIANA GREEN'S AVAILABLE BOOKS

FELICIA FISK & THE DENIZENS OF THE DARK

MISS RIDLEY & THE WARLOCK

THE FALCON'S HEART

CROSSING THE RIFT

SOLSTICE MOON

TAKING FLIGHT

HEARTH MAGE

Made in the USA
Columbia, SC
30 May 2023

799791d4-daa7-4449-be36-bb15b12db8f1R02